Serving Him
Trusting Him
Finding Him

Fairground Attractions
Ghost Train
Merry-Go-Round
Helter Skelter

Treasure Trove Antiques
The Lucky Cat
The Gilded Mirror
The Poison Bottle
The Jeweled Egg

Anthologies
Racing Hearts: Keeping the Luck
His Rules: Tagging Mackenzie

Collections
Sold to the Billionaire: The Auction Lot

Treasure Trove Antiques

THE JEWELED EGG

L.M. SOMERTON

The Jeweled Egg
ISBN # 978-1-80250-740-9
©Copyright L.M. Somerton 2024
Cover Art by Kelly Martin ©Copyright July 2024
Interior text design by Claire Siemaszkiewicz
Pride Publishing

THE JEWELED
EGG

Dedication

To everyone who appreciates
a good adventure story.

Chapter One

"Please, Sir!" Landry Carran, antique shop owner and somewhat scatterbrained submissive, turned what he hoped were appealing puppy eyes toward his Dom, Detective Gage Roskam.

"Did you or did you not bake me chocolate-dipped shortbread cookies today then eat them all yourself before I got home from a particularly trying day fighting crime?" Gage was growly.

"The cookies tempted me and, besides, what has that got to do with replacing the beads in my ass with your cock?"

"Punishment, Landry. It has to do with the punishment that you've earned by scoffing my treats."

"Wasn't the blow job I gave you a treat?"

"It was enjoyable, I have to admit." Gage reclined on the bed after thumping his pillows into an acceptable shape. "As was hearing you squeal as each of those beads disappeared into your hole."

"The last one was big! If we had a Labrador it would want that bead to play fetch with."

"So that wasn't you protesting that there should be another one then? Because I'm sure I can find a more challenging set online."

"No comment." Landry wiggled his butt, which, thanks to his position on his hands and knees on the bed, was in Gage's line of sight. "I need to come!"

"And I said you could, so long as you don't touch. I am a kind and generous Dom."

"But you won't take the cock ring off, so how can I?"

"It's quite the dilemma, isn't it?"

"You're so mean to me!"

"Are you saying you don't deserve to be punished?"

"Well…I guess I kinda do, but the cookies smelled so good, and I had to wait for the chocolate to set, which was torture. And you already spanked me…"

"Which you enjoyed, so that doesn't count as punishment."

"Irrelevant. I gave you an exceptional orgasm."

"Which you also enjoyed."

"True, but then you locked this nasty metal beast around my poor cock and tortured me for half an hour pushing silicon beads up my…"

"I know where they are, Landry. I hope they're pressing on all kinds of sensitive spots, driving you crazy… Come sit on my lap, I've got some news."

"You want to tell me something now! You're kidding me?"

"Nope." Gage patted his thighs.

"But that's going to put more pressure on my butt." Landry crawled into position. "How am I supposed to concentrate on what you're saying?"

"Focus, sweetheart. Focus."

Landry shifted, groaning as the balls inside him did unspeakable things to his prostate. "Fuck me."

"Only if you behave, listen to what I've got to say, and promise to bake me more cookies."

Landry eyed his boyfriend with suspicion. "What have you done?"

"Why do you assume I've done something?"

"Because I know you and, now Sancha's your boss, she tells me about all your misdemeanors."

Gage grunted. "She's a nark."

"She's my pal."

"Since she made detective sergeant, she's gotten way too bossy."

"So get on and take the exam, then you'll be equal again."

"She retains stuff better than me."

"You know everything you need to know inside out and back to front. I should know, I've drilled you often enough. You're scared of tests."

"Am not."

"Are so." Landry leaned forward to plant a kiss on Gage's lips. "My big, bad detective is a fraidy cat."

"I think those beads can stay in you a while longer."

Landry pouted. "I could get Sancha to arrest you for cruelty to subs."

"When I tell her about those cookies, who do you think she'll side with?"

"So not fair. What is it you want to tell me?" Landry gave a pained sigh. "Are you getting a new gun or something?"

"No, better."

"Tell me! You're such a tease."

"Okay, if you insist."

"Gage..."

"I've been asked to take part in an international exchange program, where detectives from different countries go abroad to learn new techniques and exchange ideas."

"Oh my God! That's fabulous. Where are you going and when and for how long and...do you even have a passport?"

"England. In three weeks' time for two months and yes, I do."

Landry's heart fell. "You'll be away for two whole months?"

"Will you miss me?"

I'm not sure I can cope without him for two whole months. Landry wanted to cry. His lower lip trembled. "I... Of course I will, but it's an amazing opportunity and of course you have to go." He couldn't stop it. A tear rolled down his cheek. "It's a once-in-a-lifetime thing and...and..."

"Oh, love, did you really think I'd leave you here on your own?"

"I won't be on my own. I'll have Petey and Sorrell, Mr. Lao and, and...it's only two months. Sixty days. One thousand, four hundred and forty hours." *I'm already sad, and he hasn't gone yet.*

"I'm not leaving you, Lan. I wouldn't. I get to take you with me."

"I can do it. It's one sixth of a year is all. I can... Wait, what did you say?"

"I said you're coming with me."

"To England? In a plane?"

"I think it would take a while to swim over there. The Atlantic is pretty big."

"And there are sharks and monster conger eels. You're not kidding?" Landry searched for any sign of appeasement in Gage's expression.

"I wouldn't have said yes to the trip if I had to leave you here. You get to come, too. All travel expenses and hotel costs are covered. I still get my salary plus a bonus. We only have to cover food."

Landry bounced, forgetting there was still a toy lodged in his ass. "Oh! Ooooh!"

Gage shook his head. He unlocked Landry's cock ring. "Lift up." He reached for the pull loop on the end of the beads then tugged. Each time one of the balls popped out of his backside, Landry gasped. When the last one came free, Gage wrapped his hand around Landry's cock. He gave it a few quick tugs and Landry came, squeezing his eyes shut and holding his breath. As his orgasm came to a shuddering conclusion, he let his breath out in a whoosh before collapsing on top of Gage, making them both sticky.

It took a few moments for the pleasure-induced brain fog to dissipate. "But what about the store? That was great by the way, thank you for letting me come, Sir."

"I know you like to think you're indispensable, love, but Petey and Sorrell can handle the store just fine. Mr. Lao will keep an eye on the pair of them. He won't let them get into too much mischief."

Landry hugged Gage hard. "I need to let it all sink in. England! I wonder if they're all like James Ellery over there."

"Did you have to mention that man's name two minutes after coming?"

"Sorry." Landry kissed Gage's chest. "My head's buzzing. I'm so excited!"

"We can talk about it some more after a shower. Those beads should have stretched you nicely for me."

Landry lifted his head enough to stare at his boyfriend. "If I was in any way cynical, I might suspect this was your plan all along. Fortunately, I have an innocent mind."

Gage snorted. "Innocent my ass. Get your butt to the bathroom so I can fuck the sarcasm out of you."

"Sir, yes Sir!" Landry made a run for it before Gage could decide on another spanking instead.

Even after a hot shower and another orgasm, Landry couldn't sleep. Gage of course had had no such problem and continued to snore despite Landry drawing patterns in his chest hair.

I swear he'd sleep through a zombie apocalypse. How can he be unconscious when we're going to England! There are so many things to plan, and I have questions, so many questions.

Random thoughts circled Landry's mind, and he drifted into a half-sleep state where Gage was packing parachutes in case they needed to bail out of a plane, and Landry was worrying about how much underwear to pack.

He sat bolt upright. "They have stores in England, idiot!"

"Huh? What time is it?" Gage blinked awake.

"Sorry, must have been dreaming, though I could have sworn I was awake all night." Landry checked the time. "Six o' clock." Gage's alarm went off as Landry spoke.

Gage grunted. "I have to get moving. Be a love and make me some oatmeal? I have a craving."

"I *do* make the best oatmeal in the world, but do you *have* to work? We need to talk about our trip."

"Strangely, Seattle PD doesn't allow me to drop everything with no notice to spend time with my boyfriend in order to discuss travel plans. We can talk after work. We both have jobs to do, though I know you'll spend the entire day gossiping with Petey and Sorrell."

"How very dare you! It's like you know me or something. I have big news so of course I have to share it with my friends. They will have opinions."

"Don't they always? And I have to buy coffee and donuts for Sancha before I get to the precinct because my day will go much better if she's sugared and caffeinated."

"Which is why I love her. It's my turn to get morning treats for everyone, too." Landry bounced out of bed, pulled on a pair of shorts and a T-shirt then headed for the kitchen. His work commute was approximately two minutes on a bad day. Gage had to tackle traffic, so he had to shower, eat and run. Making him breakfast was a small thing Landry could do on those days Gage wasn't hustling out the door because he was running late.

Landry measured out enough rolled oats for one person—half a cup. He never used instant oats because they turned to mush. Full fat milk made it creamy, so he put that on to simmer, sprinkling a little cinnamon into the pan. Once the milk was hot, he added the oats and gave them a good stir. Now he had to be patient— not one of his best qualities—so he bopped around the kitchen brewing coffee and sneaking blueberries from Gage's breakfast stash.

Gage appeared in the doorway. "Ready?"

"Almost. Have to add my secret ingredients." Landry stirred in a teaspoon of honey and a few drops of vanilla before ladling the oatmeal into a bowl. He scattered blueberries over the top before presenting the bowl to Gage with a bow. "It's my pleasure to serve you, Sir."

"Brat."

"Grump."

"You should have some of this." Gage ate standing up. "It's good for you and it tastes amazing."

"You know what happens if I don't wash out that bowl right away? That stuff sets like concrete. That's what's going on in your insides when you digest it. I hope you don't have to chase any criminals today because you'll be moving like a walrus on the beach. I'll stick to Lucky Charms, thank you very much."

Gage scraped the last spoonful from his bowl. "Why not eat a cup of sugar instead? And walruses are cool, have you seen the tusks on those big boys?"

"One day you will learn to appreciate the benefit of processed foods."

"One day you'll show your Dom some respect and not liken him to a one-ton mammal with fish breath." Gage put his bowl on the drainer, pulled Landry close then ravaged his lips with a breath-stealing kiss. He slipped a hand into Landry's shorts at the same time and had a good grope.

Gasping, Landry glared at Gage. "Now see what you've done!" He pushed his hard cock into Gage's body. "And you won't be here to do anything about it."

Gage chuckled. "I'm sure you'll think of something." He gave Landry's ass a smack. "Be good. Don't get into any trouble today."

"When do I ever?"

"I'm not going to credit that with a response." Gage grabbed his travel mug, filled it from the pot then departed, leaving Landry with a smile on his face and a raging hard-on.

"You and I have a date with the shower," Landry told his dick. "Fun times ahead!" He was looking forward to the day. He loved his job, had news for his friends, a trip to plan and Gage hadn't told him he couldn't touch himself. "Today is made of win! What can possibly go wrong?"

Chapter Two

Landry laid out drinks and treats next to the cash register. Mary, from the café next door, had been experimenting with some new Danish pastries and had gifted Landry some freebies in exchange for a promise of an honest review. Landry couldn't wait to tuck in, but he had to wait for his tardy staff members to show up. Sorrell arrived first, having made the trip from the top floor and the old apartment that Landry had once lived in.

"Morning, boss." He yawned.

"Heavy night?" Landry handed him his triple espresso.

"Tank is not the kind of bear who hibernates. He's quite the party animal. Took me to a new club that's opened downtown, wore me out dancing then we went back to his place where he reminded me why I'm a size queen. I got back here at four this morning."

Tank Jones, proprietor of the Coffee Bean café, and Landry's protector during part of his most recent escapade, had decided Sorrell was his. Sorrell had no objections.

"On a school night. Bad boy!"

"Two or three of these and I'll be good." Sorrell inhaled his coffee. "Where's Petey? I was worried I'd be last here."

"Coming in the door." Landry waved as his best friend staggered through the store's front door, setting the bell over it ringing. "You're late!"

"There's too much noise!" Petey moaned. "I'm gonna take the clangy thingy out of that effing bell." He had on sunglasses and his skin was pale. "Gimme." He made a grab for the peppermint tea Landry waved at him. He gulped half of it down. "So good."

"I beg to differ — that stuff is only marginally better than pond water. What happened to you?" Landry asked.

"Carson was grilling in the backyard. Our new neighbors came over, and they brought some home-brewed sloe gin. I think I overindulged. I left Carson snoring, he's not on shift today, lucky dude."

"Well, I don't care how bad you're both feeling. We have pastries to test for Mary and I have news, which will mean you both have to be more responsible." Landry swallowed some coffee then handed around the pastries. "I have blackcurrant, there's plum for Petey and bitter orange for Sorrell."

"Really? I'm not sure I can." Petey eyed the pastry like it was dangerous.

Landry had no sympathy. "You want to disappoint Mary? You've met Elton, right?" Elton was Mary's boyfriend and a similar size to the garbage truck he drove.

"You make an excellent point." Petey shoved the pastry in his mouth. "Oh, it's amazing. There's some kind of custard in here, too." Sorrell was also delighted, and Landry finished his in a few bites.

"Whoever goes for coffees next can deliver the unanimous verdict in favor," Landry announced.

"You mentioned news," Sorrell said after wiping crumbs from his lips with the back of his hand. "What's going on? Are you going on another buying trip with Mr. Lao?"

Since becoming the owner of Treasure Trove, Landry had been on quite a few road trips with the store's previous owner who had semi-retired on handing Landry the business.

"Not this time. Gage has a cop gig in England, and he's taking me with him!"

Loud squealing ensued until Petey's hangover forced him to call a halt to the racket. "Tell all," he demanded. "But quietly."

Sorrell arranged chairs by the cash desk, and they all sat down. Landry relayed what Gage had told him. "So you know as much as I do. We're going to talk more about it tonight but you two will be in charge of the store while I'm gone."

"Sorrell can be the boss," Petey said. "I'm hopeless at being in charge of anything. I had a pet goldfish as a kid and I swear that fish owned me."

"I'll be enlisting Mr. Lao to come in to keep an eye on you both, because neither of you have an assertive bone in your twinky sub bodies," Landry reassured them.

"Thank the antique gods," Sorrell muttered. "I was already stressing out at the thought of having to make any decisions."

"Hopeless, the pair of you." Landry drained his coffee. "I spy customers heading our way. Petey, fetch more drinks. Sorrell, make nice with the people. I'll check for internet orders. When it gets quiet, we can start researching all the places I'll need to visit."

"Will you be based in London?" Petey asked.

"I don't know! I didn't ask. I assume so, but I guess it could be somewhere else."

"I know you can fit the UK into Texas more than twice, but it *is* over eight hundred miles from top to bottom," Petey said. "Make sure to ask Gage tonight."

"How do you know how long it is? Never mind, I forgot you consider an atlas to be bedtime reading." Petey was obsessed with maps of all kinds.

"Texas is two-point-eight times bigger than the UK, which is eight hundred and seventy-four miles from John O'Groats in Scotland to Lands' End in Cornwall by road."

"Good to know, Petey, thanks. Where's my coffee?" Landry had priorities. Petey glared at him but scuttled toward the door. Sorrell seemed to be romancing the customers well enough, so Landry turned to his computer and was gratified to discover several new orders in the inbox. He busied himself with wrapping, labeling and booking couriers for the next hour. A steady stream of customers kept Petey and Sorrell occupied, and Landry was happy they seemed to be closing plenty of sales.

It was late morning before there was a lull, and Landry's stomach was telling him he ought to be considering lunch options when the door opened again, and the mailman arrived with a bundle of letters and parcels. Landry made small talk for a few minutes while he piled everything on the cash desk. The mailman left with a wave.

"Food first, mail second. What does anyone want to eat?" Landry yelled down the store. As if by magic, Sorrell and Petey both appeared.

"Can we get something from Basim's place?" Petey asked. "My stomach has settled and his mom's staying."

"Definitely," Landry said, licking his lips. Basim's mom visiting from Pakistan was always a local event because she couldn't resist cooking for Bas' diner. "I don't mind going."

"I'll go," Sorrell offered. "I want to stretch my legs and get some fresh air. Shall I just get whatever Bas recommends?"

"Sure. I can make a start on the mail while Petey naps." Landry gestured at one of the chairs where Petey was sitting, head back, eyes closed and mouth open. "Honestly, standards around this place are falling." Landry sniggered.

"Petey sold that scary tribal mask from Igbo in south-eastern Nigeria," Sorrell said. "He deserves a rest for getting rid of that monstrosity, because I swear the eyes followed me around the store. That thing was possessed."

"It was a bit creepy, but I guess it was supposed to be and it was quite valuable, so he can snooze for a bit."

"It went to a collector who was delighted to have found one. He'd been looking for a while apparently. People hoard the strangest things."

"Good for us that they do. Happy customers make *me* happy. You need cash for lunch?"

"I'll sort it out when I get back." Sorrell left, leaving Landry facing his mountain of mail.

"Bill, bill, flyer, junk mail... Geez, the whole save the planet message isn't getting out there quickly enough."

Landry stacked all the rubbish into a pile for recycling. "Ooh, money!" There was a check for an internet order in the heavy cream envelope Landry had just opened. He smiled. The customer was a regular buyer but didn't trust online banking. She always used checks, a fountain pen and had beautiful copperplate handwriting.

At the bottom of the pile was a small, padded packet. Curious, Landry took a closer look at the colorful postage stamps. "English! Oh..." The only person Landry knew well in England was James Ellery, and anything arriving from him usually meant trouble. Landry felt the packet. There was something small and hard inside. The postmark was from a place called Rochester. It didn't mean anything to Landry. He tore open the packet then tipped the contents into his hand.

"Well, I wasn't expecting that." Nestled on his palm was a necklace with a silver chain and a narrow silver pendant. Oblong shaped, it hung vertically from the chain and was set with seven colored stones. *Black, green, blue, pearl, black, green, pale green. What an odd combination.* There was nothing on the back other than the number nine-two-five indicating that the metal setting was definitely silver. Landry checked the packet, but it was empty and there wasn't anything to indicate it had come from Ellery. *Perhaps someone sent it in for a valuation but forgot to include a note.* Landry frowned. That wasn't likely, and the tightening in his gut told him that Ellery was somehow involved.

He debated calling Gage, but the bell over the door rang and an elderly couple ambled in. Landry shoved the necklace back in the envelope then stashed it in the cash desk before going to greet them.

"Mr. and Mr. Cawley! What can I do for you guys today?"

"Landry, you sweet boy, how are you? And call me Ferdy, like I've told you a hundred times before."

"Don't nag the boy you old curmudgeon, he's being polite, which is a rarity in this day and age." Ferdy's husband grinned, displaying a prominent gold tooth.

"Thank you, Brandon. You keeping well?" Landry asked.

"Lubricated by vintage port and sustained by fine dining, young man. I recommend it." Brandon gestured around the store. "I'm older than some of the stuff you have in here, you know, and still going strong."

"You say the same thing every time we visit. Stop your yacking and tell the boy what we want." Ferdy gave Landry a conspiratorial wink.

"We are hosting an afternoon soiree for a group of like-minded friends and need some new dinnerware. A fancy tea service, something old fashioned and flowery, like us."

Landry held back a laugh. "How many settings?"

"We're expecting twelve, plus the two of us," Ferdy said. "I like the idea of mixing two sets or even three if you have them. The more they clash the better, apparently, it's the fashion."

"You two are always on trend, and I'm sure I can help you. I have some English imports that Mr. Lao picked up at an auction." Landry guided the couple between the shelves to a table laden with vintage china. "This one is called Royal Albert Old Country Roses, and I have a fifteen-piece set including tea pot, cream jug, a covered sugar bowl and four tea plates."

Ferdy and Brandon admired the set, which featured a classic English rose motif with vibrant red, pink and yellow roses in full bloom, accompanied by green foliage and golden accents against a white background.

"I think the design is charming," Ferdy commented.

"It's not rare," Landry said. "But it is collectible. You could add to it over time if you wanted to. I get part sets in every now and again. I also have this one." He pointed out a Royal Standard tea set. "The outsides are in these lovely pastel shades, but each teacup also has a floral design on the inside. The saucers and side plates have floral designs in the center, and they all have gold detailing."

"I do love a bit of bling." Brandon picked up one of the cups. "These are perfect. We'll take the lot and the other set."

"That's great!" Landry clapped. "I'll throw in another four cups, saucers and plates I have in another pattern. I have a couple floral cake stands, too, would you be interested in those?"

By the time Brandon and Ferdy had finished shopping, they'd cleared out the store's vintage china stock. "Why don't you leave this all with me?" Landry said. "I'll get everything wrapped then we can deliver to your place tomorrow. I'll let you know the total once I've applied your loyal customer discount."

"As usual, you've come through for us Landry." Ferdy beamed. "You and that gorgeous man of yours will have to come to visit us soon."

"You just want to ogle Gage's ass," Brandon muttered.

"It *is* a fine example," Landry said, laughing. "We'd love to visit, though don't let Gage use your new cups, he has huge hands."

"All the better to deliver a spanking with." Brandon snorted with laughter.

"You can't possibly expect me to comment on that." Landry escorted his customers to the door where they were met by Sorrell coming in, his arms laden with paper bags emitting delicious aromas.

"Oh, hey, Ferdy, Brandon. Hope you spent lots of money." Sorrell gave a sweet, innocent smile.

"We did, and you're another one that needs a spanking." Ferdy sniffed the air. "I smell Pakistani delicacies. Is Basim's mom staying again?"

"She is," Sorrell replied. "If you want lunch, you'd better get down there because word has already gotten around."

Landry said his goodbyes then joined Sorrell at the cash desk. Petey, in his chair, blinked awake. "Yum, I smell food. Did I doze off?"

Landry stared at him. "Just a bit. I should dock your wages."

"Aww, Lan…be nice to me. It wasn't my fault I was led astray." Petey struggled to his feet. "What yumminess did you bring me, Sorrell?"

"Chicken kachoris, shami kebabs, aloo ki tikka, samosas and a kind of caramel egg pudding, which Bas told me isn't strictly Pakistani but is a family thing for them. It was so hard not to start eating it all while I walked back."

"If you had you'd have been risking a serious smacking. Shop picnic time, I'm hungry," Landry announced. "Then I have a new mystery to tell you about. The mail wasn't all bills today."

"I was out for half an hour, and you summoned up a mystery? Some days I think I should protect myself with a salt circle…or am I supposed to put the salt around you?" Sorrell asked as he unloaded the food onto paper plates.

"Depends if you're trying to summon a demon or protect yourself from one, I think." Petey reached for a samosa but got his hand slapped.

"Not until we're all ready to eat and I'm not a demon!" Landry protested.

"I was asleep, so whatever happened had nothing to do with me," Petey said. "Are we ready yet?"

"Dive in." Landry loaded his plate before sinking into a chair. "Petey gets to deal with any customers who interrupt lunch because he's been sleeping on the job. Oh my God, so yummy! We should ask Bas and his mom over to give us a cooking lesson so we can make this stuff when she's not here."

"It's all in the spices, so she says." Sorrell spoke around bites. "Wouldn't take nearly enough money for this lot either. She said us skinny boys need to eat more."

"For once, I'm happy to do as I'm told," Landry said with a happy sigh.

"Gage will think you're a reformed character," Sorrell replied.

"Hey! I do what he tells me. Sometimes. Okay, occasionally...when I'm tied to the bed and don't have any choice..." Sorrell and Petey both cackled. "Back to food, it's safer. How about caramel egg pudding then mystery mail?"

"Sounds good." Petey rubbed his belly. "I think better on a full stomach." He yawned.

"You fall asleep again and I'm firing you. Actually no, I need you in the store, but I'm telling Carson, and he can deal with you. You also get to dust the glass figurines."

Petey scowled. "Not sleeping. But you can blab to Carson anyway...cos that'll be fun."

Chapter Three

Landry put the pendant on the cash desk in front of his bright eyed, curious friends. "This came in an envelope with an English postmark in today's mail. There was no note or anything in with it."

"From England? That means it has to be from James Ellery, doesn't it?" Petey asked.

"Oh, is Landry going to get us all tangled up in another adventure? I hope so!" Sorrell clapped his hands.

"You know there were dead bodies involved the last three times," Landry said, putting his hands on his hips and attempting to look stern. "Actual corpses. Gage has been shot at, knocked out, I've been twinknapped more than once. I had to jump out of a moving vehicle the last time. I'm not sure I want to get tied up in another of Ellery's schemes, if that's even what this is. It could be someone sent it in for a valuation and forgot to include a note. You guys shouldn't jump to conclusions."

Petey gave him an incredulous look. "And you didn't? You don't believe the valuation thing for a minute and despite everything that happened with the lucky cat, the gilded mirror and the poison bottle, I'd wager my Las Vegas dime stash that you're just as eager to look into this as we are."

"Are you going to Vegas?" Sorrell asked.

"Can we get back to the topic of the necklace? Petey's vacation plans are not currently under discussion, though Vegas is fun, and we should all go." Landry spread the pendant out. "The chain and the setting are silver. I don't think the stones are valuable and they're an odd color combination. Not very attractive."

Sorrell stroked a finger over the pendant. "Jewels and semiprecious stones can have meanings, though. I did some research once into a piece that came into The Antiquarium. It was linked to the suffragette movement, and they used jewels in a symbolic way. The most common color combinations were green for hope, white representing purity and violet for dignity. You have two of those colors here if you count the pearl as white."

Landry snorted. "The thought of James Ellery associating himself with purity has to be way off beam. Do other gemstones have meanings?"

"I'm not sure," Sorrell said. "I didn't get much beyond the suffragettes. Get on the computer and have a look."

It didn't take Landry long to discover that a lot of stones had meanings. "I think the blue stone is lapis lazuli and it says here that it's regarded as a stone of truth and enlightenment."

"Ooh, that has to be a clue! The milky green one could be jade," Petey contributed. "What does it say about that?"

"Jade is associated with wisdom, harmony and good fortune. What do we think the other stones are? I guess the other green one could be an emerald and I think the black one is hematite. I've seen that in crystal shops." He searched again. "Oh, that has loads of different meanings. Grounding and protection, strength and courage, balancing, harmonizing, focus and concentration... The list goes on. If Ellery is trying to drop hints, he's not doing a very good job. This is a nonsense jumble of stuff. There are far too many options."

The bell over the door jangled and some customers came in. "You guys go help those people, and I'll do a bit more hunting." There was a wealth of information on the Internet about the various stones. Landry made a few notes, listing what he thought the stones were. "Hematite, emerald, lapis lazuli, pearl, hematite again, another emerald, jade." He ran a hand through his hair. "Ellery, I have no idea what you're getting at. How can you still be a pain in my ass when you're not even here?"

After that, the store got too busy for research. Landry had to clear away the detritus of lunch then had a series of sales to ring up and packing jobs to do. He'd discovered, since taking over the store fully from Mr. Lao that the manager's role included a load of administration responsibilities that he'd not been aware of, and he had to spend at least an hour a day keeping up with the banking, general inquiries and correspondence. Petey had taken on the store website and had a talent for photographing the stock to show it off at its best. Sorrell enjoyed cleaning and was never happier than when rubbing polish into antique wood.

We make a good team. Landry looked up from his paperwork. Sorrell was rearranging some vintage linens over an oak towel rail. Petey was giving customers some advice on how to wash antique flatware. Both of his friends were animated and smiling and the atmosphere in Treasure Trove had a warm, welcoming vibe. Landry gave a contented sigh. *I'm gonna miss this while we are away in England but there's no way I'm going to turn down the trip. One of the best parts of traveling is coming home.*

It was getting near to closing time, so Landry did his usual circuit of the store to check that everything was in place and note down any gaps in the stock. Petey and Sorrell trailed him, contributing suggestions as they went.

"When it's quiet tomorrow, two of us can go over to the storage facility and bring some new pieces back," Landry said. "It was a great day for sales. Could be a bonus at the end of the month for you guys if this keeps up."

"Yay!" Sorrell bounced. "I'm so glad I came to work here. The Antiquarium was okay, apart from the whole working with the mass murderer psycho thing of course, but it wasn't nearly so much fun as this place."

"Thanks, I think." Landry shook his head. "I really hope there's a simple explanation attached to the pendant. I think Gage would prefer the body count around me stay at zero."

"Is he gonna be mad about the mystery necklace?" Sorrell asked.

Landry shrugged. "He's pretty mellow. He only gets mad when I do something dumb and put myself in danger, especially if it's something he specifically told me not to do. This is out of my control, and he gets more texts from Ellery than I do. There's a serious bromance going on there, not that Gage would ever admit it. He can help me do some research with his detective skills.

He may even have heard from Ellery himself, thinking about it. Of course, if I go digging and find something potentially life-threatening, then he'll go all uber Dom on me."

"And what does that mean?" Sorrell batted his lashes.

"If it's anything like Carson," Petey said, "it means being threatened with being tied naked to the bed for the rest of my life. Carson says that a lot."

"So does Gage. I think he secretly fancies me as a sex slave."

"You'd be way too much trouble," Sorrell observed. "I don't think sex slaves are renowned for their snark."

"I'm not sure how we got to this topic, but it's time to close up," Landry said. "Petey, no drinking tonight, and Sorrell, you know you can always invite Tank to sleep over here, right? I don't like the idea of you coming home in the early hours."

"Oh, Tank always brings me. He wouldn't let me walk back on my own but thanks, I wasn't sure about having people over to the apartment, what with it being above the business and all."

"It's your home. Providing you don't wreck the place, guests are fine."

Petey chuckled. "Landry and Gage certainly got up to all kinds of things when they lived there."

"Can it, Petey!" Landry grabbed his extendable rainbow feather duster then proceeded to chase Petey around the store while Sorrell bent double with laughter.

Still cackling, Sorrell went to turn the closed sign around on the door just as Gage and Carson came in. Gage surveyed the chaos as Landry skidded to a halt in front of him, the feather duster tickling Gage's nose.

"I see things have been going on much as usual in here today," Gage muttered, pushing the duster away with a finger. "I'm not even going to ask if you've been good."

"I've been so good," Landry protested. "It's these two who've been misbehaving."

"On that note…" Petey grabbed his things, kissed Carson then pulled him out the door. "Catch you guys tomorrow."

"You go on up, Sorrell. I'll finish closing," Landry offered.

Sorrell gave Gage a shy smile. "Landry has a new mystery for you, Gage." Landry took a swipe at him with the feather duster, but Sorrell was too quick and made a run for the side door that led to the hall and stairs to the apartments above.

"Sounds like we have more than our trip to talk about," Gage said. "I hope you've been up to something I can punish you for. It's about time my hand reacquainted itself with your ass."

"So mean." Landry threw himself into Gage's arms. "I'm sure I can think of something punishment worthy." He tilted his head back, and Gage rewarded him with a rough kiss accompanied by some cheek-grazing stubble burn. "I hope you don't mind me saying but you smell a bit…rank."

"I smell disgusting. You can say it. I showered at the precinct *and* changed my clothes, but Sancha and I got called out to a body that was found in a sewage treatment plant today."

"Gross!"

"You should have heard Sancha. She was not impressed, especially when the 'body' that someone had seen turned out to be a store mannequin."

"Oh no!" Landry tried not to laugh but couldn't hold it in.

"That's right, laugh it up, brat. You just guaranteed yourself a spanking."

"Excellent! A good day is about to get even better."

Half an hour later, Gage got out of the shower, wrapped a towel around his hips then took a sniff of an armpit. "What do you think, Lan, do I still smell like sewage?"

"I used half a bottle of the expensive shower stuff your mom gave me for Christmas. You smell of freshly mown grass." Landry nudged Gage with his hip so that he could reach for a towel, too. "Not even a hint of eau de poop."

"I think I should have washed inside my nostrils because something's still lingering."

"I thought I did a super good job of distracting you."

"Stop pouting, brat. That was a superlative blow job, and if I failed to demonstrate adequate appreciation, I apologize." Gage stole Landry's towel then whipped him across the butt with it.

"Hey!"

"Don't pretend like you didn't enjoy that." Gage proceeded to give Landry a good rub down. "Gotta make sure I dry all the hidden spots, huh?"

"You're just using this as an excuse to grope me."

"Sure am. Not that I need an excuse." Gage slung the towel around his neck.

"Don't stop!"

"Demanding little…" Gage hoisted Landry into his arms. Carrying his wriggling sub into the bedroom, Gage squeezed Landry's ass. "Like a lovely ripe peach."

"Are you hungry? We should eat." Landry said. "Cos you always use food analogies, metaphors, whatever when you're hungry."

"Later. There's only one thing I intend to eat right now." Gage dropped Landry face down onto the bed. "Spread 'em."

"Yes Sir, Mr. Sheriff, Sir. Whatever you say." Landry giggled into a pillow.

"You're fucking gorgeous and you have a perfect ass." Gage straddled Landry's legs. He pulled his butt cheeks apart to admire his hole. "It never fails to amaze me how I manage to stuff my dick in there."

"I think we proved it fits," Landry muttered. "Many, *many* times."

"Always worth repeated testing in case parameters change." Gage buried his face in one of his favorite places. He probed Landry's hole with the tip of his tongue. "You taste good." Landry was already squirming and moaning. Gage gave a low chuckle then got to work, determined to turn Landry into a puddle of quivering, begging need. He licked, probed with his tongue, interspersing the main action by sinking his teeth into Landry's smooth cheeks. It didn't take long to achieve his objective.

"Sir! Gage… Please. My dick hurts it's so hard."

"Sounds like quite the predicament." Gage was already half hard but he gave his cock a few swift jerks before slathering on some lube. "Want me to do something about it?"

Landry stuck his butt in the air in response.

"Oh, that's how it is, is it? How about you say please because I like hearing you beg."

"Please, please, please, please, please! You have the biggest dick on the planet, I love you, get it in me."

"Subtle."

"You want me to crawl around the bedroom on my hands and knees? You're being so mean, Sir!"

"Maybe I should tie you to the bed so you can't touch and leave you for an hour."

"No!" Landry wailed.

Gage only grinned because he knew Landry couldn't see him. He positioned his now rigid cock at Landry's entrance then pushed home. As their bodies locked together, Gage mused on the sense of completion he always felt when he and Landry were joined. He fucked him slow and easy, building his speed in a way he could only manage because he'd already orgasmed once that evening. Beneath him, Landry muttered, "Deeper. Harder. Need it, Sir."

The need wasn't one-sided. Gage gave Landry what he wanted and shifted up a gear. The familiarity of Landry's body never got old. Gage loved that he knew how to make his sub scream. He changed his angle and Landry did exactly that. Gage reached beneath Landry's body to grip his cock. One touch was all it took. Landry came in hot spurts into Gage's hand, his entire body shaking. It was impossible for Gage to hold back. He gripped Landry's hips to get better purchase. One final thrust and he came, yelling Landry's name.

Wrung out and happy, Gage flopped next to Landry on the bed. Landry rolled onto his side to snuggle close. "I hope that improved your day some."

"Exponentially."

"Sancha has been getting you to use better vocabulary in your reports, hasn't she?"

Gage grunted. "She's banned me from writing that criminals suck. To be honest, I think she's getting above herself because they do suck. It's an accurate description."

"Good thing you get to boss me around here then, isn't it?"

"You know it. Now, I think food was mentioned. How about we order in? Not sure my stomach can wait for you to cook."

"Sounds good." Landry nuzzled Gage's neck.

"What are you after? You always do that when you want something."

"Just your opinion. I got something in the mail from England today and it's a bit of a mystery."

"James fucking Ellery. What's he up to now?" If Gage had sported hackles, they would have been standing on end.

"You're so predictable! I'm not sure he's involved. I'm trying to remain neutral. Aren't detectives supposed to keep open minds?"

"If it's mysterious and it came from England, he's involved. A perfectly reasonable deduction." Gage reached for his cell. "Any preferences for food?"

"Something we can dip into and share. How about Thai, or Chinese?"

"Thai sounds good. I have the number for The Thai Orchid. Their food was great when we had it before." Gage called then ordered a bunch of different dishes, making sure to get all Landry's favorites.

"You spoil me, Sir."

"That's my job."

"I'm never gonna disagree with that. I'm gonna go clean up."

Gage made a grab for his shorts. "I'll go downstairs to wait for the delivery."

He pulled on jeans and an old T-shirt then made his way down to the yard to wait by the gate. It was a warm night and clear, not quite dark. Only one or two stars were visible. He wondered what Ellery was trying to drag Landry into. "If that fucking Brit is up to something again, I'm gonna shoot him myself." Gage shook his head. Despite all the trouble Ellery had caused, Gage had a grudging soft spot for the most annoying Brit on the planet. He put it down to them both being Doms because he couldn't think of any other reason for it.

That man would steal from his own grandmother if he saw profit in it. He'll be onto another moneymaking scam, no doubt.

His thoughts were interrupted by the arrival of the delivery guy and his focus shifted to food. "Thanks, man." He tipped the guy then headed back inside. He had a hungry sub to feed and taking care of Landry made him happy.

Surrounded by the remains of a fantastic Thai take out, Gage examined the pendant Landry had given him. "I'm no expert when it comes to jewelry, but I wouldn't call this attractive. The color combo doesn't work. It's silver, not platinum?"

Landry nodded. "That's what the numbers on the back mean."

"Nine-two-five?"

"Yeah, it's about the purity of the metal. This contains ninety-two-point-five percent pure silver and seven-point-five percent of another metal, usually copper or another alloy. It's a standard hallmark used to indicate the quality and authenticity of silver items. I don't think it means anything else."

"Not a secret code then?"

"No, I think that might be in the stones. I was checking them out earlier and they all have meanings." Landry pushed his pad across to Gage, who scanned what he'd written.

"You're kidding me." Gage groaned. "Fucking Ellery."

"What? I know the meanings are a bit tree huggy but…"

"That's not it. Look at what you've written."

Landry stared at the list. "I don't…well, fuck me."

"That's *my* job."

"How did I miss this when you spotted it right away?"

"Because I'm a simple detective who likes to look for the obvious solutions first. You, however, have a mind like a basket of wool that's been attacked by a bunch of feral kittens on catnip."

"That's oddly specific, Gage. You've been saving that up, haven't you?"

"You can't possibly expect me to admit to it."

"Hematite, emerald, lapis, pearl. The first four letters spell help."

"What's that sneaky son of a bitch up to now?" Gage drummed his fingers on the table. "Does he *want* help with something or does he *need* help? It wouldn't shock me one bit if he'd gotten himself into trouble."

"But what about the other three stones? Hematite, emerald, jade. What the heck does HEJ mean?"

"Someone's initials perhaps? Not sure how you'd be able to work that out though, there could be millions of people out there with names that fit."

"Something else then?"

"He's hooked you, hasn't he?" Gage reached across the table to take Landry's hand.

"I can't help it! I love a mystery."

"Don't I know it?"

"Don't pretend you're not the same. Your job is all *about* solving mysteries."

"It's my job. It's not yours, and I don't want you getting mixed up in something dangerous again."

"We don't know anything yet. We just have a cryptic message that makes no sense. Besides, you might be my Dom as well as my lover, but you can't wrap me up in cotton wool."

Gage wanted to growl and assert his right to do just that. "We have a straitjacket hanging in the closet. Just saying."

"We do, but I think I'd have a tough time looking after the store wearing that, don't you?" Landry poked a chopstick into some leftover noodles. "My job is dangerous, too, you know."

"How so?"

"Have you ever dealt with someone who wants to test the sharpness of an antique letter opener? Wrestled a flintlock from a trigger-happy septuagenarian? Criminals are lame in comparison."

"I wish I'd never asked. Antique stores are clearly high risk. I need to install more cameras."

"More?" Landry stared at him. "Gage? You're yanking my chain, aren't you?"

"Think I'll let you wonder about that one." Landry pouted and Gage leaned in to give his jutting lip a bite. "What do you want to do about the pendant?"

"Sleep on it, I think. Will you try to contact Ellery tomorrow?"

"We shouldn't rise to the bait, but yes. I suppose I can send him an innocuous text then see what comes back."

"I don't have a number for Tad, or we could try him."

"Ellery keeps him well under the radar. But I have some contacts in the UK. I'll put out a few feelers. There's not much else we can do for now. We haven't talked about the trip to England. Are you okay about taking an overseas trip because if you're not happy, I'm not going?"

Landry leapt from his chair and into Gage's lap. "I can't wait! Well, I can because I have to make plans and stuff. I also have to shop for new outfits. I don't even have decent luggage."

"Do I need to hide the credit card?"

"You can spank me if I spend too much."

"I can spank you anyway, brat."

"Later?"

"There are benefits to having you bare-assed across my lap."

Landry grinned. He knew it was a certainty. "Where are you going to be based in the UK? I assumed London."

"Three different places actually. I start in London for four weeks, then two in Manchester and the last two in York. I'm on international panels at a couple of conferences along the way."

"Oh wow! Where will we be staying?"

"The Brits are organizing hotel accommodation. We don't have to worry about any of that."

"They know I'm coming with you, right? You don't have to sneak me in in your suitcase or anything?"

"They know. They're probably alerting the security services to keep an eye on you, knowing how much trouble you're apt to get into."

"Slander!"

"Is your passport up to date?"

"It has a couple years left on it. My mom always insisted me and my brothers had them, even though we didn't take vacations overseas."

"And that's why I love your mom. She's organized, efficient, never forgets a birthday…"

"And has a bottomless purse, which never fails to contain your favorite mints." Landry rubbed the back of his hand on Gage's cheek. "Hmm, stubbly. And have you noticed how she never has *my* favorite candy? Just yours."

"That's because she loves me best. She's grateful that anyone had it in them to take you in hand."

"I should be offended but you're not wrong."

"Am I ever?" Gage bounced Landry a little.

"Depends…"

"On what?"

"On whether or not my answer has any impact on how the rest of this evening goes."

"You want in that straitjacket, don't you? Tied up nice and tight. At my mercy."

"I'd love to be able to see into your mind right now." Landry nibbled his lip. "Sir."

"You know you calling me that turns me on, don't you?"

"Counting on it."

"I have a crystal-clear picture in my mind. I want you trussed up, naked from the waist down. I want you squirming with frustration while I edge you. Then I'll have you suck me on your knees before I fuck you into unconsciousness."

"Oh, oh wow." Landry jumped off Gage's lap. "You want dessert first? I have a pint of cherry chocolate in the freezer I've been saving for a special occasion."

"Bring two spoons. A sugar hit will set me up nicely for dealing with you. If there's any left, I can smear it on your dick."

Chapter Four

James Ellery checked his watch — a pleasing Art Deco Jaeger-LeCoultre Reverso — that he'd...discovered... while investigating an art smuggling operation. He knew they'd never miss one little piece. It was a little after two in the morning, and he could think of a thousand places he'd rather be than standing in soggy woodland up to his ankles in wet leaf mulch.

"The things I do for this fucking job," he muttered, confident that he wouldn't be overheard by anything other than the nocturnal creatures that seemed to inhabit the wood in far greater numbers than could possibly be normal. Yet another rustle had him glancing around to find a hedgehog snuffling near his foot.

At least it's the UK. If I were in Australia right now, I'd be dead because everything over there wants to kill you. Hedgehogs probably have poison-topped prickles. Mind you, I'd give a lot to be sunbathing on a Gold Coast poolside right now, somewhere with a clothing-optional vibe...where I could rub lotion all over Tad's smooth, naked body then...

Another noise snapped him out of his reverie. He put thoughts of his boyfriend aside and focused on the present.

His location was a corner of Oxfordshire that didn't attract tourists. No dreaming spires or gowned academics, even the local church had a squat utilitarian tower. Under cover of darkness, he'd left his car outside a hotel where it wouldn't be noted as out of place. He'd then hiked cross country for two miles to reach the ancient oak wood that now provided him with both concealment and a line of sight to a narrow lane. That was where Ellery pinned his gaze. Within minutes he was rewarded by the sound of a powerful engine as a car sped along the road. If he'd been asked to name the make, model or color he couldn't have said from observation alone because it was pitch dark and the vehicle was moving too fast. But Ellery knew it was a black Audi. He knew the registration and that the leather upholstery was claret red. Once it had passed, he stayed where he was, unmoving, for another fifteen minutes. Reassured that the coast was as clear as it was ever going to get, he hefted the small pack that sat at his feet onto his shoulders then set off down the lane in the direction the car had come from.

Moving at a steady jog, Ellery stuck close to the verge. Running on the tarmac was a calculated risk but speed was more important to him now than stealth. If the driver of that car was true to form, he'd be gone three hours, no more. That was the time it took for him to drive to a cottage in a nearby village, spend some quality time getting his ass whipped by a very expensive dominatrix, then drive home.

The things that go on behind closed doors in the early hours, even when those doors have pink roses growing around them.

Ellery smiled as he ran. He'd delivered a fair few whippings himself in his time. He didn't judge. This was nothing more than an opportunity—one he'd created through painstaking observation and a lot of hours getting cold and wet. He hoped the promised rain held off a while longer. Once his job was done, getting wet didn't matter, it would be a temporary discomfort, but if it came down beforehand would make leaving no trace a lot more difficult.

Fuck! A bat swooped in front of his face putting him off his stride. *It's rural Oxfordshire not Transylvania, get a grip.* He upped his pace, keen to get the night's work over with. He turned into a driveway, the gates wide open, jogged around a sweeping corner and where a house loomed into view. Only one window was illuminated, to the right of the front door. Ellery ignored it and switched track into the shrubbery. Slowing to a walking pace, he circled the property. He didn't expect to come across anyone because the homeowner lived alone, but Ellery hadn't stayed alive as long as he had by being reckless. 'Expect the unexpected' was a motto he lived by.

He made it to the back door without incident. The house was fitted with an alarm, but it wasn't sophisticated enough to bother Ellery. It relied on radio frequency signals sent between door and window sensors to a control system. The blocker Ellery pulled out of his backpack had cost him twenty pounds on eBay. He turned it on then set about picking the lock. It was old fashioned and simple enough for someone of his talents. In less than a minute he was inside the house and pulling the door closed behind him.

Ellery had memorized floor plans that he'd found on a property website that gave details of the last time the house had been sold. With ten bedrooms, it had many period features, including oak paneling, exposed floorboards, decorative over-mantles, architraves, staircase and studded doors, none of which interested him in the slightest. There were cross-leaded windows, some with seats, others with stained-glass panes set in stone mullions. It was one of *these* that Ellery needed to find.

Having extremely good recall for documents was useful because Ellery could picture the floor plan quite clearly in his mind. After removing his boots and leaving them on the door mat, he moved from the boot room he was in through a utility room then on to the kitchen. The cold from the worn flagstones seeped through his socks, encouraging him to move faster. When he opened it, the door from the kitchen to the hall gave a creak worthy of any haunted house. He froze, listening hard, but the house had an air of emptiness and that didn't change.

Note to self, bring a can of WD-40 when breaking and entering, although that stuff stinks, which might be a bit of a giveaway.

He padded along the corridor, ignoring doors to either side, and at the end found himself in a square hall at the foot of an impressive staircase. He took a brief pause to admire the carved oak handrail that ended in a roaring lion's head. *Nice.*

The staircase turned back on itself, but Ellery's target was above the first landing. Even in the darkness the window was impressive. Set in a stone arch, it had to be at least twenty feet high and ten across. The design was reminiscent of Tiffany and extremely intricate. Ellery retrieved his phone. He took several shots from different angles using a specialist night setting before slipping the cell back into his pack. *Time to go.* He had turned, intending to retrace his steps, when two beams of light swept across the hall, diffracted into a dozen muted colors by the glass. The crunch of gravel announced the arrival of a vehicle.

Well, that's not good. Ellery put aside his frustration that all his careful planning had come to nothing. He sprinted back the way he'd come. He had to get out, lock the door and reset the alarm before anyone attempted to enter via the front. His socked feet had no grip on the kitchen flags. He skidded around a corner, catching his hip on the edge of a marble worktop, and fell. *Fuck me!* He scrambled to his feet and made a dash for the boot room. There was no time to put on footwear. He grabbed his boots then scrabbled for the door handle. It was much darker in the small room, but he yanked the door open, lurched outside and closed it as quietly as his haste would allow, setting the latch so that it locked. He snatched up the jammer and deactivated it seconds before a blue light on the roof line started flashing. Someone had opened the front door and activated the alarm. Moments later the light stopped blinking and returned to a steady state. Keeping low, Ellery snuck across some grass into the shrubbery. Only then did he allow himself the luxury of a moment's pause.

That was a bit too close for comfort. With a grimace, he pulled his boots onto his wet feet. His sodden socks were a guarantee of blisters by the time he returned to his car. Glaring into the night, he shifted his pack into a comfortable position then edged back to the property boundary. He saw neither the house's occupant nor his car and gave no headspace to wondering why he'd returned so early. He didn't matter and had no connection to the case Ellery was working, he just happened to own a property of interest.

He's probably more pissed off than I am that his plans didn't come to fruition, knowing where he was going.

Whenever he ran cross country, Ellery was transported to his school days and a nightmare of a games teacher called Mr. Kurl. Ellery had spent a large part of that time concocting plans to get out the activity he was currently engaged in.

Old Kurly Wurly would have conniptions if he could see me now. Running voluntarily. Still, it gave me a good grounding in escape planning.

His legs got heavy, and the run seemed interminable, but Ellery eventually reached his car. He then drove another few miles to another, different, hotel. It was a very discreet establishment he'd used several times before. One where the night manager didn't bat an eyelid as Ellery left a damp muddy trail across the marble floor of the lobby at four thirty in the morning.

"Good morning, sir. Should I cancel housekeeping for you tomorrow?"

"That would be good of you, Mr. Asquith, and if you could send up a tot of your finest single malt, I'd be most appreciative."

"I'll bring it myself, sir."

Ellery gave him a weary smile then made his way to the elevator. He thought getting to his room might be preferable to losing consciousness in the corridor, but the carpet was plush and his key card annoying. He'd only just opened the door when Asquith arrived with his drink, gleaming gold in a cut-glass tumbler.

"I think you'll find this satisfactory, sir."

Ellery took the glass from the silver tray it sat on. "I know I will. Please have one yourself when you're off duty."

"Thank you, sir. That's kind. Sleep well." Asquith moved away with a lot more energy than Ellery could muster. He swallowed the whiskey in two gulps, put the glass on the nearest table then stripped off his filthy clothes. The super king-sized bed with its pristine white sheets beckoned but, despite his fatigue, Ellery had to shower before sliding between them. He wasn't going to sully that thread count by going to bed dirty.

As he stood beneath the powerful spray, he tilted his head back to let the water run over his face. The jets were hard enough to sting and to keep him awake. "I'm getting too old for this shit." He rolled his shoulders and his joints creaked and cracked. The ache in his hip told him there'd be a bruise blooming the following day.

He mulled over the events of the night. As always, his planning had been impeccable, but he'd been reminded that the fates often had a wicked sense of humor. If he'd been caught in the house, it would have been an inconvenience. An arrest for breaking and entering would soon be dealt with because Ellery had useful friends in high places. However, it would have been more of a pain to keep the story out of the papers, to buy the homeowner's silence and to cover his trail. Ellery didn't want people to know where he'd been because he hadn't been there to steal, he'd been there to look at something very particular and potentially useful.

When he was happy he'd washed away the lingering remains of his night's efforts, Ellery dried off then padded from the bathroom to the bed. The warmth of good whiskey sat in his stomach and his eyelids drooped. His hair was still damp, but he was too tired to care, even though he'd look like blond hedgehog by morning. *I've got hedgehogs on the brain.* He fell asleep with that random thought in his head.

The next day, Ellery awoke slowly, clawing his way out of sleep with reluctance. He lay still, trying to judge the time without checking his phone. The light seeping around the edge of the blinds was gray, but there was a steady hum of traffic and somewhere a dog was barking. *Must be after midday by my reckoning.* He reached for his phone and swore. Twisting aggravated his bruised hip which, when he took a peek, was mottled black and red. Otherwise, he didn't feel too bad.

He ordered room service — a smoked salmon and cream cheese bagel and a pot of strong coffee — then went to take another quick shower. This time he made the effort to style his hair. He dressed in dark wool trousers and a deep red cashmere turtleneck and was ready just as his food arrived. He accepted the delivery, locked the door then settled at a small table to eat. Once he was done and his appetite satisfied, he poured himself a second cup of coffee then rang his boyfriend.

"Hi, Tad, I hope you're being good."

"James! I miss you. Where are you?"

"Best you don't know for now, love."

"When are you coming home?"

"Tomorrow. I need to lay low for twenty-four hours before I show my face in London. Did you take care of that job I asked you to do?"

"Of course I did. I took a drive out to Kent to post it, like you said. The pendant should have arrived in the States by now. It was an odd thing to send him, do you think Landry will understand?"

"He'll work it out. It might take a while but he's curious and more tenacious than a squirrel hunting down a nut. By the time he and Gage arrive in the UK, he'll have the bit between his teeth."

"Gage is going to think up several inventive ways to kill you, you know that, don't you?"

"I can't imagine what you mean." Smiling, Ellery sipped his coffee.

"If he doesn't dismember you for fixing the cop exchange program, he'll definitely be wanting to detach parts of your anatomy for involving Landry in another mystery."

"And which parts of my anatomy might those be?"

"I quite like your balls where they are, James. I'd like them more if they were a bit closer to me."

"I'd like that, too."

"It's been over a week."

"I wonder if you would be pining so much if I didn't have the key to your chastity device on a chain around my neck."

"A week. Seven days. One hundred and sixty-eight hours."

"Your studies should distract you. Switch to video call, I want to see it." Tad's handsome face came into view. His cheeks were flushed, and his hair tousled. "Gorgeous as always, sweetheart, though I do detect some signs of frustration."

"Don't tease me. If I'm frustrated, it's your fault."

"Show me why."

"Excuse me?"

"You heard me." Tad's pained sigh sent a ripple of pleasure to Ellery's cock. Tad unzipped his jeans then aimed the phone so that Ellery could see the stainless-steel tube that encased his shaft. "Tomorrow, I'm going to fuck you before I unlock it. I'm going to drive you mad with need. I'm going to sink my cock into your needy hole and take my pleasure from you."

Tad whimpered. "James...Sir..."

"Because your body belongs to me, Tadanobu. Remember that."

"Yes, Sir."

"I have to go. I love you."

"Love you, too."

Ellery disconnected, saving his wistful sigh for when Tad could no longer hear him. "Fuck, I miss him, too." He swallowed the remains of his coffee then, after an indulgent few minutes picturing exactly what he was going to do to Tad the next day, he switched his mind back to the job in hand.

Chapter Five

"Gage, look at these cute toiletries!" Landry thrust the complimentary airline washbag under Gage's nose. "Adorable. There's even a pillow spray to help you sleep."

"Chance would be a fine thing." Gage patted Landry's knee.

"I know, I know, but it's all so exciting! I can't believe we got business-class seats. I'm afraid I'll miss something if I go to sleep."

"The upgrade *was* a nice surprise when we checked in, but you'll be exhausted when we land if you don't at least nap for a while." Gage pulled a sleep mask from the bag. "We've had the meal service. You've watched bits of at least fifteen different movies. Now you need to sleep." He put the mask onto Landry's head. "Imagine this is a blindfold."

Landry bounced in his seat. "Mile high kink. I like it!"

"Settle down, brat. The steward will be pushing you out the hatch without a parachute."

Landry pouted. "Is he there?" He reached for the mask, but Gage slapped his hand away.

"Sleep. That's an order."

"Fine."

"I'm going to lower the seat."

"Woo!" Landry yelped as his seat slid into a horizontal position. He pulled his blanket up to his chin then wriggled into a comfy curl. "Wake me if anything happens."

"What exactly do you think is going to happen? No, don't tell me. With your imagination you'll come up with something that'll give me nightmares."

"I'm gonna miss something exciting, I know it! Make sure you wake me…"

"I'm going to sleep, too, you doofus. I'm tired."

"They should have double bed seats, then we could snuggle."

"Write it on a suggestion slip."

"They have those? Where? I have so many suggestions."

"Landry…"

"Hmm?"

"Do you want your first experience of England to be a punishment?"

"Buzzkill…wait, what kind of punishment?"

Gage sighed. "One you won't enjoy. A three-day coffee ban."

"Double buzzkill. Not sure that's possible anyway."

Despite all the thoughts humming around his head like agitated honeybees, Landry did manage to doze. When he awoke, he wasn't sure if he'd slept at all or had just been hovering on the edge of consciousness. The cabin was dark and next to him Gage was snoring. Landry slipped from his seat then made his way to the bathroom to freshen up. Once he was done investigating all the buttons and cubbies, he left the cubicle and hovered, doing a few stretches.

"Hey, come back to the prep station, I'll make you a coffee." Landry's favorite air steward beckoned. Landry followed him to the compact kitchen area.

"This is how a serial killer will get me, Clancy," Landry said. "He'll lure me with coffee."

"For me it would be kittens. Or puppies. I wouldn't be able to resist even if he were wearing a ski mask and blood-splattered dungarees and carrying a chainsaw."

"It would be a good way to go. Cuddling puppies I mean, not the whole chainsaw thing because ew!" Landry took the coffee Clancy handed him. "Thanks. So how did you get into this flying gig? Do you like it?"

"Love it. I was working the front desk at a hotel where lots of cabin crew stayed. I got to know some of them, and they thought I'd be good at the job. Reception is all about problem-solving, being diplomatic and offering good service. So is this. The rest is history. What do you do?"

"I run an antique store in Seattle called Treasure Trove. I have an apartment in the same building and work with my best friends."

"Oh, I'll have to come visit. I adore old stuff — it's the ultimate recycling, isn't it? I have a weakness for vintage linen."

"Then you have excellent taste. I often have stock from Belgium, France and England. There's some amazing lacework out there if you know where to look."

"I'll definitely drop by. Do you mind me asking…who's the hunk of gorgeousness you're traveling with? Is he your husband?"

"No...he's my boyfriend." Landry preened. "He *is* yummy, isn't he? He's a detective. We've been together a while now, and he hasn't been tempted to shoot me much, so I'm taking that as a good sign of longevity."

"Oh wow! Exciting. I love mysteries on TV. I can never work out whodunit though, I get too distracted by handsome male leads and lose track of what's going on."

"Me, too. But Gage always catches me up on the plots. He always solves the crime in the first ten minutes. He's learned to not drop spoilers, though. What about you? Anyone in your life?"

"This career makes relationships difficult, but I've had my moments. Even first-class passengers love a man in uniform." Clancy grinned.

"Don't we all." Landry's mind drifted as he pictured Gage in his dress blues.

"You should get back to your seat before your man wakes up. I'll be putting the cabin lights on soon ready for breakfast service. Something tells me your Dom wouldn't want to find you missing."

Landry blinked. "And you'd be right. That obvious, huh?"

"Just a tad. He may as well have it stamped on his forehead."

Landry chuckled. "Thanks for the coffee. Let's swap numbers before we part ways. We need mutual shopping therapy."

Landry made his way back to his seat and wriggled beneath his blanket.

"You really think I didn't know you were gone?" Gage didn't open his eyes.

Landry sighed. "I tried not to wake you."

"You were gossiping with Clancy, weren't you?"

"Mebbe. Not admitting to anything." Landry snaked a hand beneath Gage's blanket. Gage grabbed his fingers and gave them a squeeze.

"I swear, if it has a pulse, you can make friends with it."

"Clancy's nice. He likes antiques so that makes him friend material. We're going to go shopping together when he has a layover in Seattle."

"Seattle's stores will be putting up the security shutters."

"Hey! I'm offended." Landry gave Gage a prod. "Are we there yet?"

"You did *not* just say that. You must have been a nightmare on family vacations as a kid."

"I had to sit in the middle between my two enormous brothers in the back of the station wagon. I had justification for playing up. Also, I was adorable."

"I'm doubling down on my belief that your mother is a saint."

"She told me I have to send her postcards. Do people still do that? She wants pretty stamps as well."

"It'll be good for you to write rather than send a text. Getting postcards in the mail is nice."

"In that case, I'll send them to everyone. I'm gonna get fun pictures, though, not touristy stuff."

The cabin lights rose, and passengers around them began to stir and mutter. "I hope that's breakfast time," Gage said. "I'm hungry."

"You're always hungry." Landry shifted his seat back into an upright position. "Tell me again what happens when we arrive."

Gage adjusted his seat, too. "Holy crap I need to stretch, these seats were designed for children, or short people." He levered himself into the aisle and began a stretching routine that had Landry licking his lips.

"It was plenty big enough for me. Imagine if we'd been in economy. It's hardly the airline's fault that you have the shoulders of a linebacker. Very nice, wide, handsome shoulders and big, sexy muscles..."

"Not the time or place, Landry." Gage glared but the passengers in the seats around them were chuckling as he resumed his seat. "Where's Clancy?"

Like magic, Clancy appeared next to Gage's seat carrying a laden tray. "You called, sir?"

"You were rubbing your magic lamp, weren't you, love?" Landry snickered.

"Is that what they're calling it these days?" Clancy deposited the tray then turned back to his trolley to serve another passenger.

"Magic lamp?"

Landry shrugged, grinning. "Parts of you are definitely magical."

Gage failed to hide a smug smile. He tucked into his breakfast. "Wow this is good, for airline food. To answer your question, even though I think I've told you this about four hundred times before, you don't have to worry about anything when we arrive. All we need to do is collect our luggage, that is my bag and your pile of pink suitcases, find a trolley big enough to accommodate them, then wheel it through customs to meet our driver. A car will take us to our hotel in central London, then we get to spend the day lazing around, catching up on sleep and enjoying the hotel's facilities until I have to go into work the next day."

"Isn't all this five-star treatment a little high-end for law enforcement?" Landry nibbled on the corner of a buttery croissant.

"Are you complaining?"

"No, just curious. It all must be costing a lot, and your department normally does things on a shoestring. They don't even lay out for soft toilet paper. I know, I've used your bathrooms, and I'm not fond of sandpapering my ass."

"Yum, crispy bacon. Your assessment of the toilet paper aligns with Sancha's by the way. I don't ask questions, I'm grateful for the opportunity when there are so many other people who could have been asked. Maybe the Brits just want to make a good impression."

"Maybe." Landry went back to his breakfast, smiling at the extra strength in his coffee, which he guessed was Clancy's doing. He wasn't convinced that all these perks were down to international relations. Something didn't fit quite right, and it was worrying away in a corner of his mind.

Still, it's London, so who cares how or why this is all happening when I get to do things I've dreamed about for years.

Once breakfast was done with and Landry had entertained himself for a while watching people trooping in and out of the bathroom, it seemed like only a few minutes before the flight was almost over and they were coming into land. Landry used it as an excuse to grab hold of Gage's hand. "My first landing, it's kind of scary."

"Are your ears popping?"

"Yeah, oh that's weird. I don't like it."

"Hold your nose, keep your mouth shut then breathe out."

"That's so clever, the pressure's gone. This is why I love you because you're so good in emergency situations."

"I don't think a perfectly normal landing constitutes an emergency, Landry."

"But my head exploding would and that's what it felt like was going to happen!"

"I stand corrected and gross. Really gross."

"I am no longer a flying virgin," Landry declared. "From here on in I count myself an experienced air traveler."

"You referring to yourself as a virgin... No, not gonna go there."

"Innocent as a newborn foal, that's me." Landry grinned. "Gee, how long is this plane taxiing for? Or is it driving us into the city?"

"Heathrow is a massive airport, I guess we landed a ways from the terminal. Sit back and relax. We'll be tackling the bedlam of the arrivals hall soon enough."

From then on, Landry followed Gage's lead, something that felt comfortable and safe. They deplaned then made their way through passport control and baggage reclaim with very little delay. Their luggage, including all of Landry's pink suitcases, was some of the first that appeared on the conveyor.

"The traveling gods are smiling on us today," Gage said as he grabbed the final case and added it to the pile on the trolley he had commandeered. "Just customs and then we are back into the real world."

"I'm gonna get strip-searched, aren't I?" Landry said. "I look guilty even when I'm not."

"To be fair, you usually *are* guilty," Gage replied.

"So not helping."

"The only strip-searching of your person that is going to happen today is by me when we get back to the hotel, okay?"

"If you say so, Sir."

Gage joined the line of people trundling their trolleys through the 'Nothing to Declare' corridor. There didn't seem to be any staff around, but Landry guessed that some of the windows in the wall were one-way and that they were being viewed from behind the glass. He had no reason to feel nervous, but he did and was relieved when they pushed through the doors into the arrivals hall.

"Wow, so many people!" Landry held tight to the trolley handle, not willing to lose sight of Gage for a moment. "I don't want to get lost. I wouldn't know what to do. I'd end up on a shelf in the lost property office."

"Perhaps I should have put you on a lead." Gage leered. "We can try that at the hotel later, too."

"Oh my God, don't! Well, do… But not now. Oh look, there's a guy over there with a card that has Roskam written on it."

Gage steered the trolley toward the man with the card. "I'm Gage Roskam, are you our ride?"

"Sure am. You okay with that trolley or you want me to steer?"

"I'm good. Lead the way."

Landry stared, wide-eyed, at everything around him. He wanted to take it all in. It might just be an airport, but it was an international airport in a different country, and everything was new. By the time they reached the car, Landry had stumbled over his own feet and the trolley several times. Their driver eyed the pile of cases. "Good job this car has a sizable boot."

"That's the trunk, right?" Landry bounced. "We have to learn another language!"

Gage shook his head and exchanged glances with the driver. "It's his first time abroad." He helped stash the baggage. "I think you've watched enough British TV shows to know all the different words for things. Now get in the car before you damage yourself."

The car was comfortable and quiet, nothing like riding in Gage's battered old Jeep. Landry stared out of the window, not wanting to miss anything, but the motion was doing its best to put him to sleep. By the time they pulled up in front of the hotel, he was flagging.

"I think I need a nap," he mumbled.

"No. Really?" Gage helped the driver get all the cases out of the trunk and onto a trolley that the hotel's doorman had wheeled onto the sidewalk. The driver had said his goodbyes and pulled back into the traffic before Landry even had a chance to say thank you.

"Guess he's on a mission." Landry trailed Gage who was tracking their baggage into the hotel. While Gage went to check in, Landry slumped in a chair in the reception area. It seemed like quite a plush hotel, lots of wood paneling and low lighting. There were a few people sitting around, some on their cellphones, some chatting and one guy, wearing a natty fedora, was concealed behind a *Times* newspaper. *Wow, people still read actual newspapers. Who knew?*

"I have the key, Landry." Gage tapped his shoulder. "The porter is already taking our luggage up."

"Okay, you may have to pull me out of this chair, though."

"I'm tempted to sling you over my shoulder." Gage yanked Landry up. "Come on, sleepy boy. Once you've had a nap, you'll feel a lot better."

Landry was half asleep already. As he passed, the man reading the newspaper lowered it and stared at him. Landry smiled at him and got a stony glare in return. He shrugged. Maybe the little puckered scar at the corner of the man's mouth meant he couldn't smile. Landry didn't think any more of it, his mind fully occupied with the prospect of a comfortable bed and a long snooze, hopefully followed by some fun time with Gage.

Chapter Six

Landry sat bolt upright. "What time is it? I have to open the store! I'm gonna be late."

"Sweetheart, you're not in Seattle, you're in London. Remember?"

"Gage?"

"Who else do you share your bed with?"

"No one. Never! London, wait, what?"

"I feel like I might need to slap your face or maybe bring you a paper bag to breathe into." Gage kissed him instead.

"Oh, that's nice!" Landry indulged in a long, slow smooch interrupted only by his stomach growling. "We're really here, aren't we? London, England."

"Well, it's not London, Ohio or Kentucky or Arkansas. There may be others but we're not in them either, unless all the folks there have started driving on the wrong side of the road."

"Don't tease me, I'm confuddled. How long have I been asleep?"

"A couple hours. I dropped you on the bed, stripped you…I don't think you noticed, you were so out of it."

"I missed you manhandling me? That's sad. Why am I so hungry?" Landry rubbed his belly.

"It's been a while since you ate properly. You had an airline breakfast, but that was hours ago. Do you want room service, or shall we go out?"

"I'm naked, Gage. I don't want to get arrested our first day here."

"You don't want to get arrested on *any* day here, but I would have recommended getting dressed first."

"I've always wanted to order room service and eat in bed. Can we do that?"

Gage handed him the menu. "Don't hold back. The bill here is covered."

"I can have anything?"

"Anything."

"Oh my God!" Landry rubbed his hands together. "You may have just made the biggest mistake of your life."

Gage sighed. "I'm regretting it already. I'm gonna take a shower. When you're working your way through the menu, pick something for me too, will you?"

"Like I'd forget. Hey, why aren't you tired?"

"Because one of us didn't spend half the night gossiping with a new friend."

Gage disappeared into the en suite and Landry shrugged. "Makes sense." He perused the room service menu then made the call, congratulating himself on his restraint. After being told the order would take around forty minutes, he flopped back onto his pillows. "This is the life." He squirmed around, luxuriating in the feel of top-quality cotton sheets and down pillows. He stared at the room phone, debating whether or not to add to his order, but noticed a flashing light. *Ooh, a message.* He pressed the button to listen to the recording.

Hey gorgeous, it's Ellery. How's it hanging? Fuck, I'm sounding like an American. I guess you're still with that half-ape detective you seem to have a fondness for. Getting him onto the exchange program was a great way of getting you over here, wasn't it? Landry gaped. *Anyway, welcome to the old country. Hope you like the hotel. I'll be in touch, sweetheart.*

Landry dropped the receiver back on its cradle like it had given him an electric shock. "Fuckety fuck, Gage is so not going to be impressed by this." He nibbled on his lower lip, trying to decide whether or not to delete the message but before he could work out how to do it, Gage strolled from the bathroom with a microscopic towel wrapped around his hips and all sensible thoughts evacuated Landry's head. His cock jerked to demonstrate its interest.

"Is that for me?" Gage grinned.

Belatedly, Landry realized that he wasn't beneath the sheets and his erection was on full display. "Maybe?"

Gage allowed the towel to drop, exposing his own similar condition. He stalked over to the bed. Giggling, Landry tried to wriggle away but Gage could move fast when he wanted to. He pinned Landry down, using his knees to push Landry's legs apart. "Where's the lube?"

"In my wash bag. Is it still in a case?"

"Don't move. Not one inch. I unpacked a few essentials already." Gage made it to the bathroom and back in seconds, brandishing the lube. He dispensed a big dollop into his hand. "Show me that ass." Landry put his arms beneath his knees then pulled his legs back. "Nice. Very nice." Gage slathered lube over his cock before thrusting a slick finger into Landry's hole. His prep was quick but efficient.

"In me. Need you." Landry was glad Gage didn't appear to be in the mood for drawn-out foreplay or teasing. He hoisted Landry's legs onto his shoulders then got into position.

"You think they use trunky over here instead of booty? Bit of word swapping? Sounds kinda weird." Gage grinned down at him.

"Really? You're an idiot. Focus!" Landry glared.

"Huh. You gotta wonder, though."

"No, you don't gotta. You oooh!" Landry's words were cut off as Gage got with the program and sank into him. He jacked his hips hard, and Landry gave thanks for a robust bed as he was treated to a serious pounding. He reached for the headboard and wrapped his hands around the rails to get some purchase. Gage seemed like a man on a mission, his brow furrowed in concentration. Each thrust was punctuated by a satisfied grunt. Landry wasn't complaining. He loved that Gage didn't treat him like a fragile little flower.

"Harder!"

"You. Don't. Give. The. Orders. Around. Here." Gage pulled out then, in a maneuver worthy of a WWE wrestler, tossed Landry onto his stomach. He hauled him onto his hands and knees then pushed into him again. "So fucking good."

"Nng." Landry reached for his cock. He was so close it hurt.

"Coming," Gage growled out the word. Landry didn't need an announcement. He knew Gage, knew his body. His cock always swelled a little more just before he came. Landry gave his own cock a squeeze. His orgasm rolled over him, inexorable, stimulating every nerve. Gage thrust a couple more times then froze as he came with a strangled moan. "Fuck." He pushed even deeper.

Landry moaned, shaking through the last throws of his release. His knees lost tension and he collapsed onto his stomach, Gage's weight pinning him down. "Love you." The sentiment was lost in his pillow.

"Just gonna stay here and squish you a while." Gage rocked his hips.

"M'kay." *There are worse places to be. Though breathing is good, too.*

Gage rolled away before the situation got critical. "Oomph." Landry shifted onto his back.

"There's something about pinning you down..." Gage pulled Landry closer.

"Power-crazed Dom, that's what you are."

"I'll take it."

There was a firm knock at the door. "Oh my God, that's room service!" Landry burrowed under the covers. The bed shifted, and Landry prayed Gage had put something on before opening the door. There was no indication that whoever had delivered the order had experienced a shock. *They're stoic over here. Probably trained not to comment on gorgeous naked men.*

"You can come out now." Gage yanked the covers back. "It's good you ordered so much because I've worked up quite an appetite."

"Where did you get that robe? It looks so soft."

"Behind the bathroom door. There's one for you, too."

"Did you bring it for me?"

Gage grinned. "Why would I do that? I'd deprive myself of the sight of you dancing across the room naked."

"Oh for…" Landry made a run for the bathroom. "While you're in a good mood, there's a message on the room phone you should listen to." Landry donned the robe then peeked around the door. Gage, phone in hand, had a face like thunder.

"He…I… Unbefuckinglievable."

"We can still eat now, right?" Landry skipped to the trolley, which was laden with food. "I got you your favorite burger." He handed over the plate, the huge pile of fries teetering. Gage grabbed a handful then stuffed them in his mouth before joining Landry at the small table.

"You're trying to distract me with food."

"Is it working?" Landry tucked into his dish of smoked salmon pasta.

"If I can have some of that garlic bread it might."

"Deal." Landry worked his way through pasta, salad, strawberries and a cheese plate before speaking again. "Wow, so good!"

"Where do you put it all?" Gage grabbed a stray cracker and a grape. "Your stomach is a bottomless pit."

"I was hungry!"

"No kidding."

"I guess we need to talk about the elephant in the room."

"More like a massive, man-eating tyrannosaurus than a cute elephant, but yeah. We do. Did you know anything about this?"

"Nope. Other than him sending me that necklace, I haven't heard from Ellery. You're the one he has the bromance with."

Gage grunted. "It's you he wants to bed."

"I don't think he'd turn down either of us to be fair. Alone or together." Landry examined a fingernail.

"Bring me brain bleach." Gage ran a hand through his hair. "I should have known that being selected for this program was too good to be true. That bastard has his sticky paws in everything. There's no escape. It explains the flight upgrade too, I suppose."

"But why? What does he need us here for?"

"Not us. You. Who knows? I don't even have my gun so I can't shoot him on sight, which I really, *really* want to do."

"How about instead, we go out for a walk to get our bearings. You need to know where the subway station is to get to work tomorrow, and I want to make sure I don't get lost without you."

"Okay. Maybe I can find a gun shop. They have those here, right?"

Landry rolled his eyes. "Get dressed, sweetheart. Ellery isn't here, and I don't think the Brits approve of guns."

Despite more grumbling from Gage, within half an hour they were in the lobby of the hotel, and Landry had procured a street map from the reception desk. He waved it at Gage. "This is much more fun than following directions on a cell. We can be proper tourists."

"Which every passing pickpocket will know as soon as they clap eyes on us."

"I don't have anything in my pocket to pick," Landry said. "And no thief in their right mind is gonna come anywhere close to you." He eyed his tall, brooding boyfriend. "Wipe that frown off your face, we're in another country with so many exciting things to see. Forget Ellery and concentrate on having a good time." He dragged Gage toward the revolving doors and the street.

Landry couldn't help but bounce a little. His nap and the good food had given him a new infusion of energy. "I've done so much research about this area. There's a ton of stuff to do around here. It's reasonably quiet during the day but apparently there's a buzz at night. I have a list."

"Of course, you do."

"Is there anything special *you* want to do, honey?"

"Can we start with you not calling me honey?"

"Honey buns? Peanut? Stud muffin?"

"Or how about the man who packed a really stiff paddle in his carry-on."

"So, *is* there anything you would like to do, Sir?"

"I'm at your disposal. Show me the sites, brat."

Landry steadied his map then turned it up the other way. "Okay. There's a massive photographer's gallery nearby, but I'll save that for a day when I'm on my own, maybe when it's raining. How about we go check out the Notre Dame de France?"

"Isn't the Notre Dame *in* France?" Gage questioned.

"I guess it borrowed the name from that one. This place is different, it was the first cast-iron church in London." Landry set off walking. "It's just down here and inside there is a series of murals by John Cocteau, apparently."

"The director?"

"Yeah, not what you'd expect to find in a church in the middle of London, huh?"

They spent a happy fifteen minutes admiring the three panels before Landry decided it was time to move on. "This will appeal to your detection skills. We have to be on the lookout for seven noses."

"I know your brain works in a very peculiar way, Landry, but I'm not so jet-lagged that you can kid me into doing something ridiculous."

"As if I would! Apparently, there are seven noses stuck to the walls around the district, so we have to look out for them. It was some artist or other that put them up as a protest against the number of security cameras being used in the area."

"I like surveillance cameras," Gage muttered. "Where next?"

"How about we grab a coffee in Soho Square? Are you hungry?"

"No, I'm still full from room service, but coffee sounds good." Gage stopped to stare into a store window.

"Since when have you been into women's lingerie?" Landry asked.

"Since never, but I think there might be someone following us and I'm trying to catch his reflection."

"Who? Where?" Landry twirled around.

"Subtle, Lan. I could have been imagining it, I can't see anyone now."

"It's a paranoid cop thing, isn't it?"

"You said something about coffee."

Landry led the way, and they bought drinks from a street stand before sitting on a bench to admire the black-and-white Tudor house in the middle of the square. "There are so many quirky things to find here. I think we should go for a stroll along Carnaby Street next."

Gage sipped his coffee. "It's a shame I won't be able to join you every day."

"Well, I thought we could save the big attractions for the days when you're free. I definitely want to see the

Tower of London and the changing of the guard at Buckingham Palace. I want to take a boat down the Thames and maybe do a ghost walk."

"Are you going to be able to fit everything in?"

"Sure I will. Some days I'll have a plan and others I'll just see where my feet take me. Do you think James Ellery will show up? Ooh, what if it was him following us?"

"Don't let your imagination run away with you. The guy I saw was older than Ellery and wearing a hat. There was something vaguely familiar about him, that's why he sparked my interest, but there's no reason why anyone should be tracking us here."

As they walked toward Carnaby Street, Landry couldn't help but be suspicious. Gage's gut had a habit of being accurate. He was trained to be observant. For a while, Landry examined people's faces and made note of anyone unusual but once they reached the bustle of Carnaby Street, he was totally absorbed by the sights and sounds around him, and any suspicions were forgotten.

Carnaby proved to be an entire area with over a dozen streets. By the time Landry and Gage returned to the hotel, Landry's feet were sore and jet lag was taking hold. He played with the new bracelet Gage had bought him. It was made from tiger's eye beads, and Landry thought it was beautiful. He'd bought a braided leather necklace for Gage and was happy Gage was wearing it. Having stopped twice for food, once for sushi and later for ice cream at a store that made it using nitrogen, they weren't hungry.

"I'm going to put on my robe and snuggle in bed," Landry announced. "I want to stay awake a bit longer to adjust to the time zone."

"Good plan. You want anything to drink from the mini bar?" Gage ambled over to the fridge.

"Just a water, please." Landry scrambled out of his clothes and into his robe. He was in bed before Gage had unscrewed the cap on the bottle. "This hotel is really cute," Landry said. "It's more upscale than I was expecting, to be honest."

"I wouldn't be surprised if Ellery had a hand in this too," Gage said. "How else would he have known where to leave a message?"

"Good point. Talking of Ellery…"

"Do we have to?"

"Yes, we do. I had a thought while we were choosing my bracelet. Could you bring me the pendant he sent, I packed it in my hand luggage."

With some reluctance, Gage rummaged through Landry's bag. "Got it." He handed it over along with a chilled bottle of water then joined Landry in bed.

"What are you thinking?"

Landry fingered the chain. "Well, I'm pretty certain the first four stones spell out HELP. Then the H and E are repeated. The last stone is definitely jade, but I realized in the store earlier where we got my bracelet, that jade is also called nephrite. That would make the last three letters HEN rather than HEJ."

"Help hen. How is that an improvement?"

"I don't know yet, but it's an actual word at least. Something else for me to work on."

"Okay, but in the meantime, I want to see you naked apart from your new bracelet. I have a paddle to try out."

Landry took several long swallows from his water. He batted his lashes at Gage. "And you'll keep your leather necklace on, too?"

Gage stripped off his clothes. "Okay, kinky boy."

"Takes one to know one." Grinning, Landry got naked before wriggling his way across Gage's thighs.

"Maybe the paddle can wait." Gage played with Landry's ass and fingered his hole. "My palm needs warming up."

Landry pushed his butt into Gage's hand. "So does my tush. Get to it…Sir."

Chapter Seven

"What is it with the fucking rain in this part of the country?" James Ellery wiped his face with a silk handkerchief then shoved it into the pocket of his jacket. Seconds later water was once again dripping from his nose as well as sliding down his neck and soaking through his pants. *I do not get paid enough for this crap.* He edged around the corner of a massive barn, giving a silent curse as he caught his arm on a rusty nail protruding from the woodwork. *Great, now I'll probably get tetanus.* A doorway provided temporary shelter, so he ducked into it to formulate some kind of plan.

That morning, he'd left a happy, sated Tad tucked in bed. By now, Tad should have followed the instructions that Ellery had put next to the kettle to pack a bag and check in to the hotel that Ellery had booked for him using cash and a false name. Tad was Ellery's weakness. If Tad was safe, Ellery could focus on the job in hand without worrying that some particularly nasty, ruthless people might get their bloodstained paws on his boyfriend.

He'd left his rental vehicle a mile or so away before hiking to the farm. It hadn't been raining when he'd set out but now it was sheeting down. Before leaving the car, he'd sent a text he'd prepared earlier.

Nothing like sharing the pain. Gage Roskam is going to detach my balls but maybe we can have an enjoyable tussle while he's at it.

Setting Landry on the same trail he'd been following was a calculated risk, but Landry had his very own pet Rottweiler to keep him safe, and Ellery needed backup in the worst way. He didn't trust any of the people he knew in his business, they'd all sell their own grandmothers for an art find, and him down the river.

An effluent-polluted river with mutant fish. Probably pike, with big teeth and no dietary issues.

The phone had gone into the car's glove compartment. He couldn't risk being caught with it.

This is a bad idea. It was daylight so not the best conditions for clandestine surveillance, but the rain had its advantages. *I need to know if Anatoly has the egg. No point in all the Sherlock Holmes stuff if I can steal it from him instead.* The rain was persistently heavy and showed no sign of easing. The sky was gunmetal gray, dimming the light. Ellery made his way across a yard awash with mud. The occasional moo from nearby sheds told him that the mud was probably a bovine by-product. *I'm wading through cow-shit. I'm a fucking idiot.* There was no sign of life. If there were farm dogs, they had more sense than Ellery and were likely somewhere warm and dry. He gave his caked footwear a wry glance.

Italian leather does not appreciate this kind of treatment. This had better be worth the effort.

He snuck around the side of a van with Elite Catering written on the side. Beyond it was a side door that stood open, wedged in place by an antique flat-iron.

"Hey, it's about fucking time you got here. I assume you're that useless pillock Steve's replacement. Get your ass inside." Ellery had had no chance to conceal himself before the man yelling at him had emerged from the doorway carrying an empty plastic crate, which he slung into the back of the van. "For fuck's sake, you're all wet. Get dried off, there are towels in the kitchen."

Ellery shrugged and did as he was told. It hadn't been his plan to infiltrate the catering team, but he wasn't going to pass up an opportunity when it offered itself on a plate. This would be a great deal easier than trying to mingle unobserved as a guest for the lunchtime function taking place in the farmhouse that day. He could be the unfortunate Steve's replacement, whoever he was.

Ellery made his way into the kitchen, which was warm and a welcome escape from the rain. Two sheepdogs were spread in front of a range cooker and, other than a slight ear twitch, paid him no mind. "You two aren't stupid, are you?" Ellery stood between them while he grabbed a warm towel from a rack next to the range and gave his sodden hair a rub. "You pooches nabbed the best spot there is." Underneath his jacket he wore a dark suit, white shirt and tie, which, though damp, were not soaked through.

"Didn't you get the memo about the dress code?" The man who'd spoken to him previously stomped into the kitchen. "I'm Flynn, and I'm in charge of this shit show today."

"It was a last-minute call," Ellery lied. "I dressed the way I usually do for this kind of gig. They didn't tell me anything, just to get my behind over here quick smart. Cab dropped me outside the property, and it was further down the drive than I thought it'd be." He pointed at his shoes. "I attempted a short cut which didn't work out."

Flynn grunted. "Thanks for making the effort. Clean your shoes with some paper towels. The dark trousers will do fine, but you'll need to put on an Elite polo shirt and a name badge. I'll fetch you a spare shirt from the van. The name badge I can't do anything about, you'll have to be Steve for the day."

"Fine with me." Ellery was quite content that he didn't have to make up a name. "What do you need me to do?"

"You're wait staff, but I need you to muck in with the unloading and plating up the canapés. Other than a few things that need warming, there's not much to do. Everything is precooked. There are some houseguests, but the rest of the party are due to be arriving from around eleven thirty. We're expecting ten or twelve people, if this fucking weather doesn't put them off."

No way would I have pulled off mixing with such a small group. My source needs a good smacking. He said it was going to be a huge party.

"In that case, I'll stay as I am while I help you unload as I'm already wet. I can save the dry shirt for later."

"Good plan. You'll be the only waiter, then there's me and a catering assistant who'll be dealing with the food prep. You'll meet her, Alice that is, when she finally gets out of the ladies' room. She's pregnant and needs to pee every fifteen minutes it seems." He pointed to a side door. "Bathroom is through there. You can leave your coat in there, too. Wash your hands before you touch anything."

That apparently was the extent of the briefing Ellery was going to get. He spent the next ten minutes trudging in and out to the van bringing in wrapped trays of food, crates of glasses and boxes of booze. Once everything was inside, he changed his shirt for a burgundy Elite Catering polo. By this time, Alice had emerged from the bathroom and set him to work unwrapping hors d'oeuvres so that she could make the plates of food look pretty with an assortment of garnish and hand-carved vegetables. She chatted away making small talk, mainly about babies, and Ellery nodded, smiled and laughed at appropriate moments.

Flynn, who had been carting bottles through to wherever the party was to take place, took him to one side. "Do you know anything about wine? Steve was supposed to be an expert."

"I can hold my own," Ellery said.

"Tell me what you know about Les Noëls de Montbenault Chenin."

Ellery frowned. "Uh, it's a very nice, well-aged chenin from Richard Leroy in the Loire, I believe."

"Excellent, what else?"

"Scents of yellow apples, white flowers, some assorted citrus fruits and nutty aromas."

"You'll do. We also have a Californian Pinot Noir for those wanting red."

"Oh, I know this one. Intense aromas of cranberry, pomegranate and cherry. Underlying notes of cinnamon, lemon thyme and sarsaparilla. An intense fruity rush. Develops on the palate."

"You do know your stuff."

"I spent some time training with a sommelier. It helps with getting the high-end gigs. Our host must be generous, he's serving great booze."

"This was one of those money-is-no-object late bookings, which are a pain in the ass but pay exceptionally well. There'll be a great tip in it for you if you do well and by that, I mean don't fucking drop anything. Smile and look pretty and don't object if one of the guests feels you up."

"If that happens, it had better be an enormous tip," Ellery muttered.

"I'll take you in and show you where everything is. Wine service first then canapés. Alice will keep them coming. Savories for the first half hour, then sweet." As he talked, Flynn strolled along a passageway then up a couple steps into a large, airy lounge room with picture windows along one wall and a grand piano in the corner. "The meet and greet will be in here then the group will move to the dining room for their meeting where you'll serve coffee and petit fours. Then we remain on standby for a further coffee order, and they're due to finish sometime this afternoon."

"Okay, all seems straightforward enough."

A small bar had been set up next to the piano. Several bottles of white wine sat in ice-filled coolers behind it whilst the red was on top. Two trays of glasses were already set up.

"Where will you be?" Ellery asked.

"Manning the bar. I'll make sure you have glasses to hand out and take any orders for alternative drinks. We have a range of spirits and soft options. I'll leave you here to familiarize yourself with the selection in case you get asked and go check on Alice."

Left alone, Ellery took the opportunity to explore the room. Other than the door he'd come through from the kitchen, there was one other exit which led to a square entrance hall. If there had been furniture in the room, it had been cleared away with the exception of some smaller tables pushed against the walls. Ellery stuck one of the two bugs he had in his pants pocket under the lip of the windowsill. The other he needed for the room where the meeting was to take place, but he wasn't sure where that was. He didn't dare wander too far in case Flynn returned. With that in mind he checked out the selection of spirits and unwrapped a package of embossed, Elite Catering coasters which he placed in a few judicious spots around the room. He was finishing off when Flynn came back.

"I'm going to check in with our host and make sure he's happy with the arrangements. Are you done in here?"

"I am. Where's the meeting taking place, so I know where to serve the coffee later?"

Flynn gestured at the door Ellery had already checked out. "Through there then directly opposite across the hall. In case anyone asks, the guest bathroom is the first door on the left at the top of the stairs." He glanced around the room. "Good job, I forgot about coasters. Bit obvious, but I don't want to miss an opportunity to get our name in front of this crowd. Recommendations are worth their weight in gold. Wait here, I want to introduce you to our host. He likes to know all the staff by name."

"Okay, who is it?"

"Oh, sorry, I forgot you don't know. His name is Anatoly Volkov."

"The Russian billionaire?"

"Like I said, the tip should be good."

"Fuck me." Ellery pretended to be impressed.

"You're not gonna act like an idiot in front of him, are you?"

"Not in the least." Ellery knew everything there was to know about Anatoly. He'd seen him once before at a London function but didn't think there was any chance he'd be recognized. Anatoly could only have seen him from a distance across a crowded room.

"This is his country place, which he uses when he wants privacy. The dairy farm is a side gig run by a tenant who lives elsewhere. There are a couple of security guys on the grounds. You can't miss them — they never seem to take off their sunglasses."

"Living up to the stereotype then?"

Flynn grinned. "Pretty much."

Ellery went to wait by the window. Outside, the rain was still bucketing down but he didn't spare a moment of sympathy for the security guys.

Definitely more luck than judgment that I didn't run into them earlier. Careless, James. Very careless.

He was still giving himself a mental spanking when Flynn returned with Anatoly. Volkov was an imposing man, his dark hair flecked with silver. His eyes were an unusual shade of pale green, and they moved constantly, taking everything in.

"Steve, I understand you're a last-minute replacement?"

"Yes, sir." Ellery made eye contact.

Anatoly nodded. "Be invisible, understand?"

"Yes, sir."

Anatoly turned away but Flynn gave Ellery a nod of satisfaction.

"Can your man take coats and collect phones?"

"He'll do whatever is needed," Flynn said.

"Good. Everything else is ready?"

"It is, Mr. Volkov."

Anatoly didn't seem to need anything further. He left the room taking a noticeable chill with him.

"A man of few words," Ellery commented.

"He expects his instructions to be followed. You picked up the bit about coats and phones?"

"Sure. What do I need to do?"

"There's a coat rack in the hall. I'll give you a box for the phones, which you can bring through here and leave under the bar so that you can start serving."

"Okay... I think the first guest may be arriving." Ellery could hear a car approaching.

"Let me get that box then I'll start pouring some wine. You get out to the hall."

When the doorbell chimed, Anatoly appeared from another room. Ellery stood to one side while Anatoly opened the door himself.

Ellery observed as much as he could whilst dealing with wet coats and a variety of expensive cellphones. Nobody seemed surprised or upset at having to hand them over, suggesting that it was the usual course of action at one of Anatoly's meetings. Ellery counted in ten guests who all arrived within a few minutes of each other. Ellery imagined it wouldn't be career enhancing to arrive late for Anatoly Volkov. He followed them through to the other room then began circulating with trays of wine, picking up snippets of conversation where he could. The topics were universally inane. The weather, the state of British roads, a play opening in London and inquiries about various wives, children and vacations. The guests were all men, all white and, without exception, reeked of money. Ellery picked up a mixture of what he assumed were Russian accents as well as British.

Once everyone had their first drink, Flynn directed him to the kitchen and he returned to circulate with canapés, keeping his eyes down and his ears open. He relayed drinks orders back to Flynn, collected empty glasses and did a good job of remaining unobtrusive. After around forty-five minutes, Anatoly clapped his hands, the conversation petered out and the group made their way across the hall to the meeting room.

Once they were gone and the door closed, Flynn gave Ellery a pat on the back. "Well done, mate. You can work with me any time."

"Thanks, that'd be great. I'll help you take everything through to the kitchen."

"Coffee's ready." Alice relieved Ellery of his burdens. "Cups are already in the room."

"Take the two pots through," Flynn said. "Pour at the side then offer them around. Cream and sugar are on the table. Bring the pots back with you." Flynn handed the tray to Ellery. "You good with this?"

"Of course." Ellery gave him what he hoped was a reassuring smile before making his way to the dining room. The door opened with a barely audible click, and no one looked at him when he entered. He listened hard over the sound of coffee pouring into bone china, but the conversation was about financial commodities.

Boring. Though I guess I might pick up an insider tip or two. My portfolio can always use work.

"Coffee, sir?" he murmured, passing quietly around the room. When he was done, he put two plates of petit fours on the table then gathered the empty jugs in one hand. Using his body as a shield, he placed the second bug under the side table, then left the room to return to the kitchen. The wireless bugs he had deployed would send recordings to the cellphone in his car, parked almost a mile away. He just had to get back there to listen.

"Any problems?" Flynn asked.

"No, they barely acknowledged my presence."

"Good, that's the way it should be. We're almost done with the clear-up."

"If you guys want to leave, I don't mind hanging around for the second coffee service," Ellery said. "It seems mad us all staying, and you guys were here earlier than me. Unless you have to wait for anything else?"

"No... But I should stay."

"I'd love to finish early," Alice said. "Junior is getting restless."

"What does that mean?" Flynn asked. "You're not going to have the baby now, are you?" Most of the color disappeared from his face.

"I might!" Alice rubbed her baby bump.

"Go! Honestly, it's just a couple pots of coffee." Ellery winked at Alice.

"All right then," Flynn said, giving Alice's belly an anxious glance. "You can leave after you've served them. The housekeeper will deal with cups and saucers."

Decision made, Ellery found himself alone in the kitchen less than five minutes later. He calculated he had at least half an hour to have a poke around the house. He did a quick check outside to make sure the catering company's van had gone. It was still raining hard. *I'm not looking forward to going back out in that mess.* He returned to the kitchen, collected the fresh coffee jugs that Alice had left then took them into the hall. Placing them on the side table, he scanned the various doors hoping for a clue as to which might be Anatoly's study. Two doors he checked proved to belong to a closet and a TV room respectively. Frustrated, he eyed a corridor that led to more rooms. He'd only taken two steps in that direction when the door to the meeting room swung open. Ellery made it back to the coffee pots quickly enough to give the impression he'd been preparing to bring them into the meeting. His heart pounded at the near miss.

"Excellent, you can bring those in now." It was Anatoly who had come out.

Ellery went through the motions of being a dedicated server for the second time, took the empty pots with him to leave in the kitchen and closed the door quietly behind him. He couldn't risk any further exploration. One close call was enough, and Anatoly Volkov was not a man to cross. Ellery didn't want to bring any more attention to himself.

He changed his shirt, his own now warm and dry thanks to Alice hanging it on the range, donned his jacket then headed out the back door, eager to listen to anything his bugs may have detected. Turning his collar up, he set off down the drive figuring any attempt at a discreet exit was pointless. The gates were open, and he paused to take a final look back at the farmhouse. The car heading his way had to be for a departing guest. He moved to the verge, cursing the long, wet grass. The car idled beside him, and the driver's window opened.

"Get in."

"Excuse me?"

"Get in the car." The driver didn't sound happy.

"I don't need a ride, thanks."

"I'm not asking."

Ellery turned toward the gate only to find two men blocking his exit, arms folded across overdeveloped chests. "I don't understand, did I forget something? I've been working with the caterers."

"We know exactly who you are, Mr. Ellery. Either you get in the car, or we put you in. Boss wants a word."

Well, shit, this isn't good. Three against one aren't odds I want to mess with.

Reluctantly, Ellery got into the back seat of the car and attempted to stay calm.

So much for staying under the radar.

Chapter Eight

Landry sat in his hotel room munching a chocolate croissant and scanning a free magazine that he'd picked up from Tourist Information. The paper was aimed at visitors and had listings for lots of events as well as advertising and some interesting articles about things to visit. He'd spent a while unpacking his cases and already had a vague plan in mind for the rest of the day but was open to being influenced by an exciting ad. Gage had left early for his orientation, and the day was Landry's to do with as he wished. It was a luxury he didn't get often, and it felt self-indulgent. He sipped his hazelnut latte then used the dampened end of his finger to pick up the last flakes of pastry from his plate.

The Natural History Museum had been on his bucket list for forever, and he was also keen to visit the V&A because Mr. Lao had recommended it. Gage wasn't that interested in museums, so Landry didn't feel bad about visiting without him. *But which to choose?* The Natural History Museum currently had a 'Wildlife Photographer of the Year' exhibition, an annual showcase of stunning wildlife photography from around the world. Landry was excited to see the pictures and learn about the challenges faced by the photographers who captured such unique moments and to see the funny pictures that were exhibited as well as the more serious ones. *Cute fluffy things or…* An ad for the V&A caught his eye. There was a special feature on there that was due to finish in a week or so called 'Fabergé in London: Romance to Revolution'. It was an exhibition exploring the connections between the Russian jeweler Carl Fabergé and the British royal family, as well as the wider context of the period leading up to the Russian Revolution. The exhibition showcased a range of Fabergé pieces, including iconic Easter eggs, jewelry and other intricate objects crafted by the Fabergé workshops. Landry loved anything sparkly.

The dates of both exhibitions meant that it made much more sense to visit the V&A and save the Natural History Museum for another day. *Decision made.* He sent a quick text to Gage to let him know where he was going.

Off to see bling at the V&A. Love you!

Gage immediately replied.

Living the dream! Be good.

"Why does he always feel the need to tell me to be good? I'm always good." Landry stuck his tongue out at his cell. By his calculations, it was about two and a half miles from the hotel to the V&A. It was a nice day and still early so he decided to walk so that he could take in a few other sights along the way. If he got tired, then he'd travel back via the subway. *Though I have to get used to calling it the Tube.*

After packing his satchel with a few essentials and clutching his map, Landry made his way outside. He stopped to chat with the hotel's doorman, Winston. They'd met the previous evening and were already on first-name terms. Landry knew that Winston was from Trinidad, had three children, a wife who was a pediatrician and that he was learning Japanese on Duolingo. He'd been in the UK for five years and missed the Caribbean sunshine. He'd recommended the best restaurant in London for authentic jerk chicken.

"Morning, Landry, where are you off to?" Landry outlined his plan for the day. "That sounds good. My other half likes to window shop at Tiffany and Cartier." Winston chuckled. "Window shopping is all it'll be unless we win the lottery."

"You never know. Sometimes the strangest series of events works out for the best." Landry had a lot of experience in that area.

"Sounds like there's a story we need to share over a drink."

"Definitely! Let's make a date when I get back."

Winston beamed. "Deal. Have a great day."

Landry's phone pinged with a notification. "Probably Gage checking up on me already." He shrugged then took a seat in the lobby. The message was from a number he didn't recognize. He was tempted to ignore it, but his curiosity got the better of him. The picture that opened was of a stained-glass window. A big one. *That makes zero sense.* It was pretty but meant nothing to Landry. *I guess it was sent by mistake.* He put his cell back into his satchel and set off.

Walking proved to be a good choice. His route took him the entire length of Hyde Park and Kensington Gardens where he took a break by the Peter Pan fountain. To his utter delight, tame parakeets came and sat on his shoulders. He took a dozen selfies, sending the best one to Gage and to Petey and Sorrell back in Seattle. He had no idea what time it was back home, but Petey responded immediately.

Why are there parrots in London?

Parakeets and no clue.

Landry googled it while he continued his walk. By the time he reached the entrance to the V&A, he'd discovered several urban myths about the parakeets that meandered through Jimi Hendrix, a hurricane, filming of *The African Queen* with Humphrey Bogart and a burglary at George Michael's home. They were all more romantic than the probable reality of escaped pets with voracious sex lives.

When he tripped up the entrance steps, Landry decided it might be wise to put his phone away. He gaped at the imposing façade then made his way inside to pick up a guidebook. "Holy crap this place is huge!" he exclaimed, getting a few amused glances from other visitors. The guidebook told him that the museum covered twelve-point-five acres and had one hundred and forty-five galleries. He headed for the café to make a plan.

Twenty-five minutes, one fruit scone and two coffees later he had mapped out a route that took him along a trail called 'Out in the museum' which would show him objects revealing stories of diverse gender and sexual identities. It took in all the areas he wanted to see most, ending up at the Fabergé exhibit.

He was fascinated by androgenized portrayals of Buddhist figures and fell a little bit in love with a bronze relief depicting a polyamorous relationship in the 1930s. There were a ton of religious artifacts that showed ambiguities around sex and gender had been around for centuries. "Wow, the Hindu gods knew how to party." Landry leaned in to examine some phallic markings on a little statue. Further on his route he got to see the Progress Pride flag and then an equally colorful snuff box that had belonged to Frederick the Great who, according to the notes, had been both effeminate and lascivious. Landry grinned. *Go Freddy!*

In the jewelry room, he found a brooch by an American metalsmith made in response to the Aids crisis, confronting the anguish of survivor guilt. Landry allowed himself a snivel before moving on. There were so many fascinating things to see that he resolved to come back again another time. The Fabergé exhibit was in a room next to the jewelry displays, and Landry lost himself in the fanciful designs. His favorite was a pendant called the 'ice crystal' on loan from a foundation in Houston. It could have been worn by a character from *Frozen*, one of Landry's favorite films. He took a bunch of pictures and drew the attention of a guide who came over to him.

"Stunning, isn't it?"

"Sure is. Weird I came all the way from the States to see something that lives over there usually. Though I guess Houston is about as far from Seattle as here is."

"Do you prefer the jewelry or the eggs?"

"I love it all. The eggs with things hidden inside are the best, though."

"Did you know that some of them are missing? There's a big mystery surrounding their whereabouts."

"Wow, really?"

"Do you have some time? I could tell you about it."

"Sure, I'd love to hear the story." Landry wasn't bullshitting. Gage would love hearing about a mystery.

The guide, whose name was George, had to be in his eighties. Landry was happy to sit next to him on a cushioned bench. His legs were feeling the effects of a long walk anyway.

George clearly relished his captive, willing audience. "So, I guess you already know a little bit about the House of Fabergé. It was founded by Gustaf Fabergé in the nineteenth century and the most famous eggs were produced for the Russian Imperial family as Easter gifts."

"The ones you have here are incredibly intricate," Landry said.

"The craftsmanship is amazing," George agreed. "Between 1885 and 1917 a total of fifty-two eggs were created, and every single one was unique. They were made with precious metals, gemstones, enamel and they often contain surprises or hidden compartments."

"Jewelry meets engineering," Landry commented.

"Indeed. During the Russian Revolution in 1917, the Romanov dynasty fell and the Imperial treasures, including the eggs, were seized by the new Bolshevik government. They sold some of them to raise funds and some of the eggs ended up in private collections and in museums around the world."

"They must be worth a fortune."

"Priceless, really. How do you put a monetary value on a unique work of art?" George scratched his head. "Over the years, several of the eggs went missing. Some could have been lost or destroyed while others were secretly sold. The time after the Russian Revolution was unstable to say the least."

"Hasn't anyone ever tried to track them down?" Landry asked.

"Of course. Very occasionally one resurfaces at an auction and that's big news in the arts and antiques world."

"I run an antique store myself, in Seattle. I'll have to keep an eye out."

George chuckled. "Well, you never know. The Necessaire egg was discovered recently. It was acquired by a scrap metal dealer in the States who intended to melt it down for its gold content. Luckily, he got curious, and it was identified before he liquefied it."

"Wow, close call."

"Sure was. There was another one called the Alexander III commemorative egg which was rediscovered in 2002 and sold to a private collector. So they do come up."

"Which ones are still missing?" Landry was intrigued.

"You sure you don't mind listening to an old man blathering on?"

"I don't know what blathering is, but I do want to hear."

"Okay, you asked for it. There may be others, but one of the most famous is called the Royal Danish egg, which was created for the Dowager Empress Maria. It was topped by the symbol of Denmark's Order of the Elephant and inside were portraits of the Empress' parents. Another one is called the mauve egg, which was given by Tsar Nicholas the Seventh to his mother.

There are only vague descriptions of that one, but Fabergé's invoice described it as a mauve enamel egg with three miniatures which were of the tsar, his wife and their oldest child."

"Sounds cute."

"There's another one called Cherub with Chariot, but only brief descriptions exist. They suggest it was a gold egg covered in diamonds and sapphires being pulled by a chariot and an angel with a clock as the surprise inside it. But, if you want cute, you'd probably like the Hen with the Sapphire Pendant egg. That one's a bit of a mystery, but the surprise in the egg was almost certainly a hen, covered in gold and rose diamonds, taking a miniature sapphire egg out of the nest, which was also covered in diamonds. That one made it to the Kremlin because it was included in an Inventory in the early 1920s. After that, nobody knows."

Landry's mind was working overtime. "A hen?"

"Yes. If you search online, you'll probably find more information."

Landry got to his feet. "Thanks so much, George, this has been fascinating. Tell me, are there any stained-glass exhibits here?"

"There's a Tiffany display. Beautiful stuff, though glass isn't my special subject." George gave him directions to a room that wasn't far away, and Landry headed off.

This is way too much of a coincidence, but I wouldn't put it beyond James Ellery to be on the trail of a missing Russian treasure. It wouldn't be the first time he's pretended to be Indiana Jones. How many jeweled hens can there be? Something to look up later.

When he reached the Tiffany room he gasped. The area was dark with benches in the center and the pieces, which included a range of art nouveau glass by various artists, were backlit to show them at their best. The effect was spectacular. Landry gaped at the rainbow of iridescent colors. He wandered around in a daze, wondering how each artwork could be more beautiful than the last. Louis Comfort Tiffany had a dedicated area, which showed several lamps, vases and mosaics. There were also two full-size, reproduction windows in the back. Landry got closer to read the information about them. One was a copy of the tree of life window, significant because it was the last window Tiffany designed; the other was a contemporary reproduction of a window called Landscape in Light from 1917. It was this one that looked remarkably familiar to the image on Landry's phone.

He took a seat in the center of the room and pulled out his mobile to compare the two images. *They're almost identical.* From what Landry could discern, squinting at the small screen, there were two differences. In the bottom, right-hand corner of his picture were three hens pecking at the ground and in the top right, a tiny coat of arms.

Holy shit. I need to get back to the hotel so I can do more research.

It was only when Landry got to his feet that he became aware of another person in the room, sitting at the other end of his bench. Though the man had his gaze pinned on the exhibits, Landry thought he'd moved.

He's been watching me, I'm sure of it. That hat is familiar, too.

He couldn't be sure, but he thought it might be the same man he'd seen in the hotel lobby the previous day. *Try to look casual.* He wandered the room, not wanting to seem like he was rushing away. He sauntered out of the exit then increased his pace to the end of a gallery. He edged through another door before turning to take a peek. The man in the hat was heading his way. Landry made sure he was out of view then gave up any pretense of being relaxed. He ran, full tilt, through several rooms, drawing quite a few annoyed exclamations.

Finding the exit proved a challenge, but once outside he shot across the road and hid behind a broad-trunked oak. Fedora Man emerged from the museum a minute later, scanned the street in both directions then shrugged. From his vantage point, Landry was able to confirm that it was the man who had scowled at him in the hotel lobby. He was just able to make out the little scar at the corner of his lip. Landry stayed hidden until the man strolled off in the direction of the subway. His celebrations were short-lived because Landry soon realized that the man didn't need to follow him because he knew where Landry was staying.

As a precaution, Landry walked to a subway station that was a little further away. He didn't feel like exploring anymore. He wanted to get back to Soho, find a cute café with vast quantities of pastries then settle down to some serious research. He debated texting Gage to tell him about Fedora Man but decided not to.

There's a guaranteed spanking in my future and it's all James Ellery's fault.

Chapter Nine

With hindsight, Landry realized that not immediately telling Gage he had been followed had been a mistake. A really big, painful mistake.

"Ow!" As the paddle made contact with his sore ass for the sixth time, and not in a fun way, Landry was rethinking a lot of his life choices.

"Okay, punishment over, brat. I hope you've learned your lesson?"

Landry did a naked wriggle into Gage's lap and nuzzled his neck. "Yes, Sir. I'm sorry, Sir. I've made a note to always tell you right away when I'm followed by a creepy dude in a hat with a scarred face at a British museum." He licked Gage's earlobe.

"Do I need to spank you again?"

"What? Why?" *Maybe I should have been a tad more contrite.*

"Don't sound so affronted, you know exactly why."

"Fine." Landry pouted. "I will tell you straight away whenever I get followed by anyone, anywhere."

"Yes, you will. After our previous adventures, you should know better than to keep anything like that from me."

"I didn't want to worry you at work. It was your first day, and you need to make a good impression. Also, I don't want your new colleagues to think I'm some kind of needy dependent boyfriend who can't be left alone for ten minutes."

"It's my job to worry about you." Gage gave Landry's hair a tug. "It comes with the Dom territory. Plus, you have a track record."

"Uh, so do you! Subs worry, too, about all kinds of things. I worry that you've got on clean underwear, that you're eating right, that some raving lunatic is going to try to kill you…"

"Point taken. I always wear clean underwear, though."

"I was fine, I just got a bit spooked is all. He didn't do anything. It might have been a coincidence anyway."

"The chances of it being coincidental that some random dude shows up in our hotel lobby and in the same room as you in a massive museum are slim to none, Landry Carran, and you know it. I swear, I am going to spend a long, pleasurable evening killing James fucking Ellery when he next shows his face near me."

"It's tempting, I know, but what about Tad? He needs his Dom."

"Okay, not killing then. Maiming. There are a few body parts he can do without."

"So bloodthirsty. What if Ellery's in trouble? He obviously wants my help and after today, I'm convinced he's on the hunt for this missing Fabergé egg."

Gage held Landry close. "If he's on the trail then others will be too, and if it's worth as much as you say, that kind of money attracts some very bad people. People I don't want you anywhere near."

"But I..."

"Landry, I swear I will lock you in chastity for the rest of your life if you don't do as I say."

"That doesn't sound like much fun." *He'd do it, too!*

"Neither does dredging you out of the Thames."

"If I had on a metal cage, you could go magnet fishing and pull me out by my dick."

"Magnet fishing..."

"You know, where people drop strong magnets on a line into the water and pull out bombs and shopping carts and bicycles and stuff."

"I know what it is, Landry. Honestly, your mind is baffling. I want you to take your safety seriously."

"You sound grumpy. How about you fuck me? That always makes you smile."

Gage dumped Landry on his back then made a lunge for his suitcase. Before Landry could ask about Gage's questionable packing choices, he found his mouth stuffed with a ball gag. A blindfold followed. Then all he could do was feel as Gage stuffed another orifice. He punctuated his thrusts with a series of commands.

"You. Will. Obey. Me."

Holy fuck, this is hot!

"You. Will. *Not*. Pull. Bombs. Out. Of. The. River."

Landry thought Gage might be missing the point in the throes of passion.

"No. Getting. Dead."

Though this orgasm may kill me... The gag didn't allow for more than a muffled scream, but Landry did his best as he came.

"Fuck!" Gage followed close behind. Screams of pleasure were a great motivator for him, even muted ones.

They both collapsed in a sticky, messy heap. Gage pulled the gag free, leaving Landry grinning from ear to ear. "You're quite good at that, you know?"

"Quite?" Gage groped for Landry's cock and gave it a squeeze.

"Quite excellently brilliant. The master of all orgasm deliverers. The commander in chief of cumming. The emperor of ejaculation. Can I stop now?"

"Dear Lord, please do."

"Can I take the blindfold off?"

"I suppose."

Landry pulled it free then tangled his legs with Gage's. "Can I tell you about today's clues?"

"I need a shower first, then food. If my brain has to deal with Ellery's conundrums, I need fuel."

"Fair enough." After returning from the museum, Landry had found a busy café in Covent Garden and done some research into the stained-glass window and the coat of arms. He was itching to share what he'd found with Gage and get his input. "You do think better on a full stomach. What do you want to get?"

"Nothing fancy. How about we take a walk and find some street food?"

"Not room service?"

"No, I could do with some fresh air. I was stuck in meeting rooms most of the day, and though it was all interesting, I get a bit stir crazy when I can't get out."

"You miss hunting down bad guys."

"It's different, is all. Sancha and I are in and out of the precinct all the time. I'm not used to sitting still for so long."

"Street food it is!"

After quick showers, they left the hotel and took an aimless amble around the area, not looking for anywhere in particular. In was fun to explore side streets and discover interesting corners. Other people seemed to have the same idea because a lot of places were busy but, in the end, they opted for a stall selling Indian food, which had a covered seating area alongside it. They tucked into samosas and bhajis followed by the most delicious curry Landry thought he'd ever tasted, scooped up with freshly made naan. Gage sipped an ice-cold Tiger beer while Landry settled for a soda. When they were done, Landry took out his cell and pulled up the photos that had to have come from Ellery.

"The hens can't be a coincidence, even I'm not that dense," Landry said, pointing out the difference between the picture Ellery had sent and the original. "Three hens. The interpretation of the pendant. A missing egg with a hen in it."

"You're not dense. I think you have to be on the right track with this Fabergé egg, it's exactly the kind of thing that would spike Ellery's interest. He seems to be getting you to follow the trail he's already on, which worries me."

"Why?"

"Because it suggests to me that he thinks he might come up against some problems and needs backup. Did you find anything out about the coat of arms?"

Landry was insulted. "Did I...? Do bears like a cuddle?"

"I consider myself reprimanded."

"You so should. Yes, I tracked it down. It belongs to a family called Ascott. The name seems to date back to the Norman Conquest when it was Aucourte, but it gradually got anglicized. There's some long, irrelevant history until the early 1800s when the family began to accrue wealth from trading...in Russia."

"Ah, make sense. So you have another good connection. Who are the descendants?"

"That's the odd thing," Landry said, "the family seems to have died out completely. The only information I can find on people of that name are obituaries and the last is quite recent. It said that Edgar Ascott died in a tragic accident and left his entire fortune to animal charities. He had no surviving heirs. His only child, Giles Ascott, died of a heroin overdose two years ago. Edgar lost his wife to cancer ten years ago and neither of them had siblings. He was the end of the line." Landry picked at the remains of a samosa. "It's kind of sad."

"It's kind of suspicious," Gage said.

"What do you mean?"

"You're a sweet, innocent soul, Lan, and I love you for it, but think about it." Gage had his detective face on. "If this family was in possession of a valuable lost treasure, which they'd kept secret for this long, they were in the way of whoever wanted to get their hands on it."

Landry put his fork down, his appetite gone. "If you're right, that means two people have already been killed over this."

"At least two." Gage frowned. "There could be more."

"What if Ellery is next?" Landry was on the verge of tears.

"That miscreant knows how to look after himself. I'm more concerned that someone is aware of your connection to him."

"I don't get it."

"You're being followed, Lan. The only possible explanation is that someone knows Ellery has been communicating with you and has been covering their bases. They may not have known exactly what he sent you…"

"Then I gave it away by visiting the V&A today. I'm an idiot."

"Not an idiot, sweetheart, just over-endowed with curiosity and a desire to help out one particularly annoying Brit."

"Sorry." Landry's lip trembled. "Can we go?"

"Sure. We paid already." Gage left some coins on the table for the young girl scurrying around clearing tables. "I'm taking you to bed. I feel the need to fuck the guilt out of you. This is not your fault, love."

Landry examined the checked paper tablecloth. "Maybe."

"Definitely. But for the next few days you're going to be a normal tourist. I want you to bore the pants off anyone following you around."

Gage pushed his chair back decisively then with a comforting arm around Landry's shoulders, marched Landry back to their hotel.

* * * *

For the next week, Landry did what Gage had told him to. He became the perfect tourist. He trekked around all the sites and at the weekend, when Gage was off work, they ticked off some of the big-ticket spots. At the Tower of London Gage admired the dungeons, they went to Madame Tussaud's because Landry wanted to pose with all the waxworks of famous people and they watched the changing of the guard at Buckingham Palace where Landry spent some time considering what the soldiers kept under their giant furry hats. Landry also found time to fit in some of the antique stores Mr. Lao had recommended to visit to introduce himself and he filled his cell with new contacts. He even took a boat trip down the Thames on a river taxi thinking that it would frustrate anyone trying to follow him.

He kept an eye out for men in hats but didn't spot anyone for a few days. It wasn't until he was out feeding the ducks on the Serpentine in Hyde Park when he spotted him again. Wearing the same fedora hat, he was half concealed behind his newspaper, sitting on a bench next to the water. Not bothering to hide what he was doing, Landry took a picture then sent it to Gage, though there wasn't enough of the man's face visible to identify him. If he saw Landry taking the picture, he gave no indication. Annoyed that the man had managed to track him down again, Landry spent the rest of the day touring sex toy shops in Soho just for the hell of it.

The next day, Gage took Landry out for an early breakfast. In London you could eat your way around the world, and, after a bit of research, Gage had found an Italian place with amazing pastries and aromatic coffee.

"You spoil me," Landry said, having devoured two chocolate bomboloni.

"I do and sometimes you deserve it." Gage sipped thick black coffee. "Your shopping trip yesterday was worthwhile. That new leather paddle you found was inspiring. It had a really nice snap. I'm definitely going to invest in some more of that bondage tape, though I think I'll go for black not pink."

"I think it's brilliant that it sticks to itself but not to me. Who had that idea? Inventors amaze me. Do you think whoever it was had plans to tie up his boyfriend at the time?"

"I think there may be other applications for the stuff, love."

"I bet he did." Landry gulped the last of his coffee. "Those sort of plans focus the mind."

"However it came about, it's good stuff. Made a change from using rope or cuffs."

"I'm glad you enjoyed yourself." Landry licked his lips, tasting coffee. "I did, too."

"The sounds you made left no room for doubt," Gage said. "I'm surprised we didn't get a call from hotel management because they'd had a complaint about the noise."

"I'm not that loud!"

"That's okay. I brought several nice gags." Gage checked the time. "I have to go. I won't tell you not to go out and about today, but I don't want you going anywhere where there aren't a lot of people. Do something touristy again. I'm going to have a word with some people at work about you being followed. I'm also going to look into the deaths of the Ascott family to see if anything suspicious was noted."

Landry shifted in his chair. His backside was a little sore after the previous evening's activities.

"I feel like I've wasted good research time this week. Fedora Man must have been following me, even though I didn't see him."

"Keeping yourself safe is not wasting time," Gage scolded.

"We haven't heard anything else from Ellery since he sent me the picture. I hope he's okay."

"If he wasn't, I'm sure he'd find a way to let us know," Gage grumbled.

"Well, I thought I'd go check out the British Library. I can apply for a free reader pass that's good for a year. It will get me access to their reading rooms and online resources, too."

"A library sounds safe enough." Gage sounded dubious. "You could find trouble in a monastery, however."

"That's slander. Or libel. Or something, I don't know. Trouble finds me, I don't go looking for it."

"No, James Ellery does that then leads you by the hand right into it. He and I are going to have words. Detailed, explicit words."

"All bromances go through rocky patches."

"I am not in a bromance with that crumpet-munching, stiff upper lipped, wannabe Columbo."

"I don't think Ellery is much like Peter Falk. He's more couture suit than tatty raincoat. How about James Bond?"

"No."

"Albert Campion."

"I have no idea who that is, but also no."

"You're spoiling my fun."

"Not in any way sorry, and I really have to go. I want you to call or text me every hour. If you don't check in, I'll send the cavalry after you."

Landry pouted. "I can look after myself. I'm all grown up, you know." Gage didn't say anything, just gave Landry a look of utter disbelief. "Hey! I know how to adult. I do." Landry fiddled with the paper airplane he'd made out of his napkin. "Okay, maybe not quite there yet."

"Every hour, Landry." Gage pushed his chair back. "Don't make me remind you. And tonight, you and I have a date with some restraints and a reminder about how Dom-sub relationships work."

"Ooh goody! My memory is bad."

"Not bad. Selective." Gage planted a kiss on Landry's lips.

"It's like you know me or something," Landry muttered. Gage grinned before walking away, leaving Landry with a pang of longing. It was exciting being in a new country, but Landry would have much rather spent more time with Gage. The weekend had been far too short but the pleasant soreness in his ass was enough to keep him going for a while. He ordered a hot chocolate to go and checked directions to the British Library.

Two tubes in the rush hour convinced Landry that he'd rather walk ten miles than go down there again during peak commuting time. He texted Gage before he went into the library, *Tubes are stinky*, then set about the process of working out where to go and what to do. After a conversation with a helpful librarian, clearly accustomed to soothing confused foreigners, Landry found a quiet corner of a reading room to continue his research into the Ascott family. He was proud of himself for remembering his hourly check-in with Gage, which earned him responses with an increasingly strange variety of emojis.

He fell down a few rabbit holes that led nowhere and had to order himself to focus. He imagined Gage giving the commands, which helped a lot.

Frederick Ascott, Edgar's grandfather, had returned to England from Russia during the Russian Revolution and from what Landry could find, had never gone back. Around that time, the family had been the registered owner of two properties, a townhouse in Chelsea and a house in an Oxfordshire village, which Frederick had had built.

If Frederick brought the egg back with him, it could be hidden in either of those places. Would that be too obvious, though?

Landry explored sales records of the Oxfordshire property and found it had changed hands several times. When he drilled into the estate agents' websites, he found pictures in the archive.

Nice place. Oh! That's the stained-glass window in the picture Ellery sent me. I'm on the right track. Is there something else in the window? No matter how hard he looked, Landry couldn't find anything else. *So, the window links the egg to the family but not that location. Ellery wouldn't need help if it was that easy.*

Landry switched his attention to the Chelsea townhouse. He confirmed the family link when he found the coat of arms carved into the lintel above the door. The family had lived in the property until the death of Edgar Ascott, at which point it had been put up for sale for an eye-watering amount of money. The buyer had purchased via a company, which Landry tracked to the Caymans but after that the trail went cold.

His stomach rumbled. *Time for snacks.* He checked his cell for somewhere close by. *I'll take a quick break then come back later. Snacks will boost my brain power.* He sent Gage another text,

Snacks are calling.

He got an eye-roll emoji back in response and stuck his tongue out at the screen.

I'll be putting that tongue to better use later.

How does he do that? Landry eyed the latest message from Gage. He packed his satchel then set off for a nearby sandwich shop.

Having bought a ham roll and a giant chocolate-chip cookie, Landry found a bench and settled down to eat and people-watch. He sent a picture of his cookie to Gage. He found himself checking out passersby for the man who had followed him the previous day, but if he was around, he was doing a great job of concealing himself. Food gone, Landry stood, intending to return to the library, though he had doubts about how much more information he'd be able to find. His cell alerted him to a message, and he paused to check it, expecting it to be from Gage. It was from an unknown number.

"We need to meet," Landry muttered. "Ookay."

Who are you? He tapped in response.

"It's a tad cool today." *Tad?* Landry debated how to respond without using a name but before he could think of anything another text arrived.

Stroked any lucky cats lately?

Where and when?

Your hotel. Half an hour.

Landry wasn't far from a subway station—he had enough time. He messaged Gage to let him know he was going back to the hotel. *How does Tad know where we're staying?* He didn't have time to puzzle that one out. He had places to be.

When Landry got back to the front of the hotel, hot and a bit out of breath, a powerful motorcycle pulled over alongside him. The rider, dressed head to toe in skintight black leather, held out a helmet. Landry couldn't see the rider's face through his visor but rammed the helmet on his head, adjusted his satchel across his body, then mounted the bike behind him.

Tad, I hope this is you or Gage is going to kill me and put my corpse in chastity so I can't enjoy the afterlife.

He wrapped his arms around the biker's slender waist and held on tight.

Landry had always been scared of motorcycles. A skateboard was more his speed. He closed his eyes as his chauffeur wove through traffic in the hectic London streets, keeping his speed down.

"Landry, if you don't loosen your grip, I'm going to die." Tad's voice filled Landry's helmet.

"Ooh, that's clever! I can hear your voice."

"The miracle of Bluetooth. Arms, Landry."

"Wow, fussy much." Landry loosened his grip a fraction. "Your ability to breathe is less important than me not falling off this oversexed crotch rocket."

"Would you rather ride the bus?"

Landry gave that some serious thought. "No, fedora scar lip dude could follow me on the bus. Where are we going?"

"Your thought processes are extremely difficult to follow. We're not going far, don't worry."

"Don't worry, he says. Not far, he says. Mr. Sexy-mysterious-leather-dude." Landry muttered.

"I can hear you, Landry."

"Oh yeah, I forgot. My bad." Landry clamped his mouth shut. He risked opening his eyes and was surprised to find that Tad was driving down a slipway next to the river. He turned off the ignition and put the bike stand down. Landry clambered off then struggled to escape his helmet. Tad dismounted with a great deal more grace. He unzipped his jacket before removing his helmet, shaking out black hair that was longer than Landry expected.

"Gage said you had short hair."

"I forgot you've never seen my face." Tad ran a hand through a few tangled strands.

"I've seen the rest of you." Landry had witnessed Ellery giving Tad a whipping back in the States.

"We made quite an impression that night at Scorch, didn't we?"

"And in the video Ellery sent Gage."

"Mmm, that was a fun night. I can see why James has a thing about you."

"He does not!"

"I think he'd like to tie us together then have Gage fuck you while he fucks me."

"He... I..." Landry didn't know where to look. The opaque waters of the Thames became fascinating.

"You can dream about that tonight. Share the fantasy with your detective."

"Why are we here, Tad? What do you want?" *Why does he have to be so gorgeous? This is so not fair.*

"Down to business then. You're right, we can talk kink another time because I think we're going to be buddies."

"Lord help me."

"It's a bit late to be finding religion. I need you to help me find James."

"Have you mislaid him? That was careless."

Tad shrugged off his jacket, revealing a skintight T-shirt sporting some strategically placed rips.

That looks like a rag so it probably cost a fortune.

"He can be difficult to keep track of."

There was a low wall that ran along the edge of the slipway. Landry examined it for creepy-crawlies then parked his butt. He patted the section of wall next to him. "Okay. Take a load off. I have a feeling this may take a while."

Chapter Ten

Landry was a little surprised when Tad did as he suggested and took a seat next to him. Black leather molded to Tad's thighs, and Landry spared a passing thought for how he'd managed to get into the pants without causing himself an injury. "Why don't you start from the beginning? This is all about a missing Fabergé egg, isn't it?"

"James knew you'd work it out. He said you wouldn't be able to resist a puzzle."

"Oh, did he now? I have a lot of questions about why he felt the need to involve me at all, Gage has even more, but I'll stay quiet." Landry waggled his fingers. "Speak." He side-eyed Tad, taking in his dark green eyes and aquiline nose. *No one has any right to be that pretty.*

"Okay, so James has always had this thing about hunting down hidden treasures. He keeps files on his computer containing research about missing artworks, buried hoards and stolen artifacts. Everything from fabled pirate bullion to gold looted by the conquistadors and legendary Samurai swords. He has searches set up that trawl the web for any tidbits of information. He adds to the files every time he sees something of interest. Every now and again he'll get excited about some random article or blog post and he'll start digging. He can get obsessed."

"Sounds like Gage when he's on a case," Landry muttered. "He eats, drinks and breathes the investigation until it's solved."

"The process is probably not dissimilar. The kind of treasure hunting James does is detective work of a sort, though the crimes were usually committed a long time ago. Once he gets the bit between his teeth, James is… Persistent. He always says he's careful, but he has been known to skate along the borders of legality."

"No shit. I have personal experience of his lack of respect for law and order, remember?"

"Yeah, I forgot about that. My bad."

"You're forgiven. Carry on."

"James had been working on another insurance case, hunting down a ruby bracelet that had been taken from a hotel safe. It was owned by a Brazilian popstar but originated from czarist Russia."

"I don't think I heard about that on the news," Landry commented. "I think I would remember."

"It was kept really quiet. The hotel was here in London, and the event that had been taking place, when the theft occurred, was a fundraiser for a political party. Neither the hotel nor the organizers wanted any publicity for obvious reasons. The great and the good of London and international society were at that event. They wouldn't have taken kindly to interrogation or any suggestion that someone on the guest list was a thief. Anyway, to cut a long story short, James recovered the bracelet. When he found it, it was in its original period box and the inner lining had come away a bit at some point during the theft. James found a letter hidden under the lining."

Landry was thoroughly engaged in Tad's story. "What did it say?"

"I'm getting to that." Tad rolled his eyes. "It was a love letter, written in Russian, from a woman who signed herself Yelizabeta, to a man called Frederick. In it she thanked him for the beautiful gift, describing how much she adored the hen inside the egg."

"Oh my God, that's proof that the egg really did exist!"

"It's a bit of a jump to assume that it was a Fabergé egg she was referring to, but James took a leap of faith. The letter was dated February 21, 1915."

"It could have been a Valentine's gift," Landry said. "Was Valentine's Day a thing back then?"

"I asked the same thing. According to James, the earliest possible origin story of Valentine's Day is the pagan holiday Lupercalia. Something about fertility, stripping naked and whipping."

"You're shitting me."

"James always finds a kinky angle to everything and so did the Romans because apparently Lupercalia was popular and one of the few pagan holidays still celebrated one hundred and fifty years after Christianity was legalized in the Roman Empire."

"Rome equals Gladiators. Yum." Landry had the DVD box sets of the entire series of *Spartacus*. They were well watched.

"Focus, Landry. Some Pope put an end to it and soon after, the Catholic Church declared February 14 to be a day of feasts to celebrate the martyred Saint Valentine. So, yeah, it was a thing back then."

"Wow. Okay, so this Frederick dude got his paws on the egg then gave it to his lady friend. That has to have been Frederick Ascott, doesn't it?"

"You have been busy. That's what James was working on. Frederick left Russia before Yelizabeta, probably to get things set up here for her to follow him. She was killed not long after."

"Oh no! That's so sad. I guess we wouldn't have a missing egg if everything had gone to plan."

"It was quite a tragedy. But, it's possible that she gave her most prized possessions to Frederick to transport, knowing how dangerous the situation in Russia was getting. James was following Frederick Ascott's trail."

"Which took him to the house with the stained-glass window?"

"I'm impressed."

"Ellery sent me a picture of the window. It wasn't that hard to track it down."

"I didn't know that he'd sent that," Tad said.

"I'm supposed to be on the best vacation ever and instead, I'm trekking around London on research trips being followed by some creepy dude in a hat, and Gage is starting to get antsy about the body count attached to the history of this thing."

"Woah, slow down there. You mentioned this guy before. You're being followed?" Tad swiveled around but there was no one in view unless people on boats on the river counted. "And body count? What the fuck, Landry?"

"Does James tell you anything important?"

"He's…protective." Tad frowned. "Especially so this time round. He must have been quite worried."

"Doms."

"Uh-huh."

"Think we're incapable of taking care of ourselves."

"Don't I know it?"

Landry gave Tad an update on his mystery stalker, on what he'd found out so far and what Gage was doing to help. "So there you are. You know everything I do."

"I'm not surprised Gage is getting fidgety."

"I'm lucky he didn't lock me in the hotel room and rent a couple Dobermans to sit outside in the corridor."

"What a fucking car crash. I swear, I should be the one tying James to the bed, not the other way round." Tad's knee bounced until Landry put a hand on it.

"Much as I like the idea of Ellery being immobilized, we have more immediate issues to deal with."

"Like where he is."

"Exactly."

"James owns a flat in Chelsea. I live there, too. He uses it as a London base and the last time I saw him was there."

"How long ago?"

"Almost a week now."

"So only a couple of days after he sent me the picture of the window."

"It's not unusual for him to disappear for a while. He travels a lot with his job and sometimes he has to go off grid. This is a bit longer than usual, though."

"What do you do? Do you have a job?"

"I'm studying for a PhD and I do some work on the side, security checking company systems. I'm usually home most of the time, but he told me to check into a hotel for a few days, so I don't know if he's been there. He would have come to the hotel, though."

"What was he like when you last saw him?"

"Completely normal. Attentive. He always is when he's been away because he feels guilty for not looking after me better. We had a great few days...he'd, I mean...I was kinda frustrated and it was great to see him."

Landry bent double laughing. "He had you in chastity, didn't he?"

Tad's pale cheeks colored. "Stop laughing. You're a sub, you should be empathetic."

"Just glad it wasn't me. He hasn't left you in that...predicament again, has he?"

"No, thank Christ, but he didn't tell me where he was going, only that he'd be a few days at most. It's past that and I'm worried. He would have been in touch if he could even if it were only a quick, cryptic text message."

"He hasn't contacted me or Gage either. He left a message on our hotel room phone and he has my number because he sent me the picture of the stained-glass window. I know he texts with Gage — those two only pretend to hate each other. I've been playing tourist for a few days because Gage wanted me to bore the guy who's been following me into giving up."

"I sent you the pendant — James asked me to do that."

"He arranged our hotel, too, didn't he? And he got Gage onto the exchange program."

Tad shrugged. "Yeah. He wanted a way to get the two of you over here. It's a great hotel. The place the police would have paid for was a concrete cube on a main road. You'd have died from some hideous lung disease if you'd stayed there sucking in exhaust fumes."

"Delightful."

"What are we going to do, Landry? I don't have a clue where to start."

Landry wandered down to the water's edge. "There must be all kinds of hidden treasure under there. Wrecks and stuff."

Tad came to stand next to him. "There is. This is a good spot for mudlarking. What has that got to do with finding James?"

"You need to tell me what mudlarking is, because it sounds kinky." Landry tossed a small pebble into the river then watched the ripples spread. "We need to get beneath the surface. If James is after the egg then other people must be, too. We need to follow the money."

"Okay, how?"

"I need to talk to Gage. Is there somewhere you can meet us this evening? Somewhere we won't be followed. Then we can plan our next steps together because if I don't involve him, Gage will make sure I never have another orgasm and I'm too young to die."

"Dramatic much?"

"Orgasms are the stuff of life, Tad."

"Have you ever heard of The Underground, the club, not the subway?"

"You can't be a true kinkster and not have heard of it. It's one of the best BDSM clubs on the planet."

"James and I are members. I can set up guest passes for you and Gage. How about we meet there tonight at nine? The security there is pretty tight. Lots of members prefer to be private about their activities."

Landry bounced. "Really? That would be awesome! I mean, it sounds like a great place to meet and discuss important things, but I've wanted to go there for *so* long."

Tad shook his head. "I hope Gage can keep his mind on finding James because you're going to be off down a dungeon rabbit hole as soon as you walk through the door."

Landry patted Tad's shoulder. "Try not to worry. Gage and me make a great team and this isn't our first mystery."

"Could we keep the dead bodies to a minimum this time? James takes great delight in telling me about your adventures."

"No corpses. Check. I guess you should take me back to Soho, unless you wanna hang out a bit longer?"

"I'll drop you a bit away from the hotel. We shouldn't be seen together too much, or I'd definitely show you some of the more interesting parts of London."

"I'm intrigued!" Landry followed Tad back to his motorcycle. "You can tell me more on the helmet speaky thingy."

"How does Gage not shoot you?"

"Hey! I'm adorable."

Tad grunted as he slung a leg across his bike. "You're a small target, it must be that."

Landry clambered on behind him. "That's heightist! Drive, lanky one, I need brain fuel to deal with all this complication."

"What's that, omega fish oil or something?"

"Coffee, smart-ass. And possibly a donut."

Tad revved the bike. "Possibly?"

"Definitely. Sue me."

Tad dropped Landry off two streets away from the hotel. He bought take out coffee and a bag of donuts at the nearest café then walked a deliberately circuitous route, sipping his coffee and window shopping. Winston caught sight of him as he approached the hotel and Landry stopped for a chat.

"Winston, would you mind if I talked to you about something? I can pay in donuts." Landry shook the bag, noting the grease soaking through the paper. "They're fresh and still warm."

"How could I refuse an offer like that? I'm due a break. There's a bench over there — go take the weight off while I drag my replacement out here."

Landry commandeered the bench before anyone else could grab it. Winston joined him less than five minutes later and handed over a bunch of paper napkins. "Greasy donuts are the best, but I don't want to get marks on my uniform trousers." He spread a few napkins over his lap. "Payment in advance."

Laughing, Landry handed Winston the bag and Winston tucked in. "Fair enough."

"So what do you want to talk about? You look worried, and I don't like it when my favorite guests aren't having a good time."

"I've been having a good time, but I also have a missing friend, and someone's been following me."

"Nothing like diving straight in there, Landry. What on earth have you gotten yourself into?"

"Sorry. It's kinda complicated."

"Give me the potted version."

"The what?"

"Summarize."

"Oh, right." Landry gave a very quick account of what was going on. Winston listened, ate and didn't say a word until Landry had finished.

"Well now, that's quite the story."

Landry grabbed a donut from the bag before Winston could eat them all. "I'm not making it up."

"Did I say that? That story is way too wild to be made up. This creep that's been following you, does he wear a hat and have a scar by the corner of his mouth?"

"Yes! That's him."

"I see everything in my job. He's been hanging around a lot. Sits in the lobby behind a newspaper."

"That's the one. He was doing exactly that on the first day we arrived, but I was so jet-lagged I didn't take much notice. I thought he was a bit grumpy is all."

"Do you know who he is?"

"No, but he has to be tangled up in all this somehow. I've been being a good tourist recently, letting him follow me around to his heart's content, not that I see him that often. He must be sick of me taking pictures of statues and old buildings. But now I know my friend's missing, I need someone to run interference for me. I have to do some things I don't want him to be aware of. I was wondering if you might...?"

"Say no more. I'm in."

"You are? Oh wow, that's fantastic! I don't want you risking your job or anything."

"A guest asks, we do. This is the most excitement I've had in months. At least since the affair of the missing pink squirrel costume."

"Excuse me?"

"Furries, man. They get up to all kinds of shit."

"I...got nothing."

"Leave it with me. He won't cause you a problem from now on."

"You're not a hit man, are you?"

Winston rolled around laughing. "You Americans are so funny!"

"Hey! All the best criminals are British according to the movies."

"I'm from Trinidad! Does that man of yours know what you're up to? I won't do this unless he's in on it. He's a policeman, isn't he?"

"Detective. Yeah, Gage knows everything, and I'll tell him about you this evening. He'll probably come talk to you, but I wanted to get you on board first. You're *my* friend."

Winston beamed. "I need to get back to work. You tell your Gage to come talk to me this evening before I go off shift at seven."

"Coolio, he should be back before then. Thanks, Winston, I really appreciate it."

"Nobody messes with my guests." He smiled warmly. "Or my friends." Winston got to his feet. "And thanks for the donuts. If you ever get to meet my wife, you don't tell her how many I ate, okay?"

"Deal." Landry high-fived his friend then followed him into the hotel. Back in his room, he texted Gage to warn him that they had a date that night then spent a luxurious hour soaking in the bath. Self-pampering was essential before a visit to a club like The Underground.

Chapter Eleven

Landry stretched out on the bed and stroked Gage's upper arm. "Love your muscles."

"You only want me for my body."

"Well...you do have a very nice body." Landry petted a few more areas, enjoying himself. Then he screamed and squirmed as Gage tickled him.

"I come in from a hard day, and you're lying there, on display, wearing nothing but a tiny thong." Gage placed a hand over Landry's growing bulge.

"Are you complaining?"

"Not complaining, but you've been busy today and we should be talking, not messing around." Gage stripped off the T-shirt that he'd had on under his shirt.

"Ooh, yum! Messing around sounds great to me. Did you talk to Winston on your way in?"

"I did. He's a good man, and worried about you. As am I."

"You didn't tell him not to help. Did you? He was kinda excited about the whole thing."

"Against my better judgment, no, I didn't. He has a few good ideas for keeping the guy in the hat off your back and the more people looking out for you, the better. You should have talked to me about it first, though."

"Sorry, Sir." Landry pasted his best contrite expression on his face.

"No, you're not, brat."

"You caught me, Sir. What are you going to do about it?" Landry rolled onto his stomach, displaying his ass. Gage slipped a finger beneath the slim strip of satin separating Landry's butt cheeks.

"You know I can't resist when you wear these. Though how anyone has the nerve to call them underwear I'll never know. More like 'hardlythere'."

"That would be a great brand name," Landry said. "Perhaps we should start our own line of kinky underwear."

"We have jobs." Gage pulled the thong to one side so he could finger Landry's hole. "Lubed and ready for me. Very nice. Did you have fun getting yourself prepped?"

"Enemas are not fun, Sir. Also, I didn't come and I need to, so bad. I missed you all day."

"Even when you were plotting with Tad?" Gage slid his finger into Landry's channel.

"You never told me how beautiful he is. Oh!" Gage crooked his finger and Landry squirmed. "Do that again! No wait, my dick is squished!"

Gage smacked his rump. "Get on your hands and knees and un-squish yourself then."

Landry scrambled to obey. The bed dipped as Gage straddled him, and Landry held his breath. He let it out in a gradual, satisfying exhale as Gage entered him, slow, steady and familiar. "I love you so much."

"If you can still form words, I can't be doing this right."

Gage proceeded to correct the situation and soon it was all Landry could do not to scream. He reached for his aching cock. "Come to papa!"

"Come before I do and I'll take you to The Underground with a lead attached to your dick," Gage muttered as he increased the speed of his thrusts.

"So mean!" Landry gasped. He squeezed his shaft hard in an attempt to stave off orgasm and lurched to one side as he overbalanced.

Gage caught him and, having almost slipped free, pushed deeper into Landry's body. "Trying to get away from me?"

"Never."

Gage chuckled, the deep sound sending vibrations through Landry's body. "That's right. Never letting you go."

"Please! I can't... I need..."

To Landry's vast relief, Gage came with a satisfied grunt, stilling, his muscles trembling. Landry didn't wait for permission. He gave his dick a quick pull then squeezed his eyes shut as the pleasure-pain of a delayed orgasm rolled through him. "Holy fuckety fuck!" He lost strength in his limbs, but Gage held him tight and kept him safe. Landry lost himself in the moment and when he regained his senses, he was snuggled into Gage's side, drooling a little onto his chest.

"Sorry." He dabbed at the wet patch.

"You were so out of it."

"Good choice of words. That orgasm was spectacular. I think I had an out of body experience."

"I'll take that as a compliment."

"You should. Thanks for not dropping me."

"Have I ever?"

"No…no. You always look after me." Landry snuggled closer and Gage stroked his hair.

"Always will."

Landry gave a happy sigh. "Much as I'd love to stay here until we're ready for another go 'round, we need to eat. Get ready to go out."

"This wasn't how I envisaged our first trip to The Underground," Gage said. "We should be going to have a good time, not for a clandestine meeting."

"It's not the trip I daydreamed about either, but it doesn't have to be the only time we go, does it? It's a great place to meet Tad because it'll be private. He said the security there is on the ball and unless Fedora Man is a member, he's not getting inside if he does manage to follow us."

"Security would need to be tight. Members of gay BDSM clubs don't tend to court publicity, and The Underground is in Westminster, really close to the Houses of Parliament, Westminster Abbey and the Supreme Court. It wouldn't surprise me at all if The Underground has a fair few high-profile members."

"Kinky politicians and judges. Fun!"

"You have strange ideas about entertainment."

"More importantly, what shall I wear?" Landry petted Gage's chest hair.

"Well. I'd suggest another one of those thongs and nothing else if it were just me, but because you'll be on view, maybe a cassock or astronaut suit?"

"Crazy man. How about we compromise with leather pants and a mesh T-shirt?"

"Plain T-shirt, no mesh."

"You've never minded other men looking at me, so long as they don't touch. Though this possessiveness is turning me on."

"Usually, I like showing you off, but tonight, I need to concentrate. You looking too sexy would be a distraction."

Landry preened. "That works both ways. You should wear saggy jeans and that God awful Blue Öyster Cult T-shirt that I know you will have packed, even though it's only fit for cleaning the Jeep."

"That's my favorite T! It's vintage."

"It's a rag."

"Can you honestly tell me that you won't be distracted by every other man in the club? You'll be so excited you won't be able to sit still. I could walk in there in a pink tutu, and your eyes will still be everywhere else."

"And now I'm picturing you in a tutu."

"You ever, *ever* mention that to Sorrel or Petey, or God forbid, James fucking Ellery, and you can say goodbye to orgasms for the rest of your life."

Landry held back a laugh. "Yes, Sir. Understood. No discussing the tutu."

"I'm fucking doomed, aren't I? You'll tell Petey, Petey will tell Carson and then the entire Seattle fire department will know. It'll get back to Sancha, and so will the police department."

"I like orgasms too much," Landry said. "Your secret is safe with me."

"What secret? It was just an example."

"Strangely specific, though…"

Gage huffed but ordered room service while Landry took a quick shower. He made Landry wear a bathrobe while they ate. "You sit there in a towel or less, and we'll never make it to The Underground."

"I could call Tad and put it back a bit?"

"No, he might not see the message if he's already on his way."

"True. Did you get anything useful back from your colleagues at work today?"

"A bit. Not much. Let me get ready then I'll tell you in the cab on the way."

"'Kay. You want the rest of those fries?"

"Go for it."

Landry happily stuffed his face with salty goodness and ogled Gage while he got ready. *Sometimes I can't believe how lucky I am.* "You're gorgeous." Gage gave him the kind of smile that could melt the pants off him. "Don't do that!"

"What?"

"That. Look at me like you want to spend the entire night nailing me to the mattress."

"Any flat surface would do." Gage shimmied into a pair of snug black jeans without putting any underwear on.

Landry gulped. "Is it hot in here? Maybe turn up the AC."

"Something to keep your mind on me instead of other men." Gage pulled on a dark green T-shirt then tousled his hair with a minimal amount of gel.

"I hate how you can look so good with so little effort," Landry grouched. "And why would I ever want to look at another man when I have you all to myself?"

"There's no harm in looking. I'd be shocked if you didn't."

"You don't. At least, I've never noticed you eying up anyone else."

"You're all I can handle, sweetheart."

Landry flung himself into Gage's arms. "I love you so much!"

"I know it. I love you too, despite the fact that you're still not ready to go out. I could fit in a quick spanking before we leave…"

"No need!" Landry shed his robe and was dressed in less than a minute.

"Impressive." Gage smirked.

"I was motivated."

"Let's go find Tad."

In the hotel lobby, there was no sign of Winston, nor of the man in the hat. Gage hailed a cab within a minute, and they were soon on their way south toward the river and Westminster. Landry snuggled against Gage's side and got a wink in the rear view from the cabbie.

"Tell me about work. What did the Brits have to say about the deaths of the Ascott family?"

"Nothing was noted on the case records in either case, father or son. However, that doesn't mean there wouldn't be interest in taking another look if something new came to light. Giles Ascott had some history as a junkie. He'd been caught in possession of methamphetamines but not heroin, which is what he OD'd on. You said that Edgar Ascott's obituary mentioned a tragic accident as cause of death."

"Was it a car crash?"

"No, nothing that ordinary. He was walking beneath some scaffolding, which collapsed. He sustained a serious head injury and never recovered."

"That seems plenty suspicious to me!"

"Only because you have different parts of the story. Both deaths seem perfectly innocent in isolation."

"Did you tell them why you were interested?"

"Only that you were doing some research into the family's connections to Russia and were curious about them dying out."

"I can't help but think that it's all a bit fishy. My gut doesn't like it."

"And considering the amount of junk food your gut can deal with, that's a worry."

"Are you casting aspersions on my diet?"

"Tell me, have you ever met a pastry you didn't like?"

Landry gave that serious topic appropriate consideration. "I'm not keen on anything with sultanas in."

"Oh, well that's okay then."

"They look like bunny droppings and, though bunnies are cute, I don't want to eat their poop."

"I'm not sure how we got here, but I'm backing out fast. What were your impressions of Tad?"

"He's clever and pretty and snarky. He's perfect for Ellery. He's also worried about him, more than he let on, I think. He also rides a motorcycle likes its part of his body and can really pull off a pair of leather pants."

"Do I detect a note of envy?"

"He's six inches taller than me. If he donated half of them, I could reach the top shelves in the store without needing a step stool."

"But then you wouldn't be able to rest your chin on my shoulder."

"Good point."

"And your ass wouldn't be at the perfect height for me to…"

"Gage!"

"You're perfect as you are. You don't need to be taller."

"Okay." Landry pouted but was secretly pleased. "I think Tad's right to be worried. Ellery wouldn't leave him alone for so long without letting him know why. He's a Dom."

Gage grunted. "He probably doesn't like letting Tad out of his sight for any length of time. I'm inclined to agree. I think Ellery has got himself into some deep shit."

"So he'll need us to come to his rescue."

"This isn't a game, love. We need to be careful and involve the proper authorities."

"And by the time they get their asses in gear, Ellery could be wearing concrete underpants."

"Shouldn't that be cement shoes? Though I wouldn't object to his dick being entombed forever."

"I think you spend too much time worrying about what Ellery does with his dick."

"Only when he's waving it in your direction, and I mean that metaphorically."

"Still, it can't hurt if Tad and I do some more research, right? We can't get into trouble hitting the books."

"Landry Carran, you could get in trouble watching TV. I'm withholding judgment on what's safe until we've spoken to Tad."

Landry would have protested but the cab drew up outside an innocuous building down a Westminster side street. "Oh my God, we're here. I'm so excited!" He tumbled out of the cab, almost landing on his ass on the sidewalk in his hurry. Gage paid the fare then gave Landry a stern look.

"Behave. Try to remember that you're my submissive."

Landry stared at his feet. "I won't let you down. I want to make a good impression here, too."

"I know you do and I've no doubt you will." Gage took Landry's hand before leading him into a building marked by a discreet plaque and two, less subtle security guys. Landry was reassured by their presence. He was also pleased to find Tad waiting for them next to a reception desk.

"Hi, Detective Roskam, thanks for coming. Hey, Landry."

"It's our pleasure, Tad, and call me Gage." Gage approached the desk where a young redhead got him to sign a visitor's book.

"Your sub will need to wear a collar, sir, to show he's not looking for a play partner."

Landry noted that Tad was already wearing one. He shivered as Gage buckled the leather strip around his neck and his cock perked up. When Gage cupped his cheek with his warm hand, Landry leaned into the touch.

"Like that, don't you?" Gage asked. "We should consider something more permanent very soon."

"Oh!" Tears welled and Landry's face heated. "I'd like that," he whispered. He touched the collar, wondering what kind Gage might like to see him wearing long term.

Tad's eyes gleamed in the glow of soft lighting. "You two *are* good together. Ellery said you were made for each other, but I didn't really believe it until now."

"He said that?" Landry was going to cry.

Tad nodded. "He talks about you guys all the time."

"Can we go in now because I need a stiff drink?" *Why did I say stiff? So not helping.* Landry needed something else to think about before he made a spectacle of himself by bawling all over the lobby.

"You'll be having a soda, but yes, let's go in. Lead the way, Tad, as we're your guests." Gage gave Landry's hand a squeeze.

Landry squared his shoulders in an attempt to pull himself together. He didn't want to let Gage down and going into such a famous club looking like a sniveling wreck was not going to help.

They had to ride an elevator down to the club, which was below ground. When the door slid open and they walked out into a space which was much bigger than Landry expected, he couldn't help but gape. From where he stood, he could see a stage, a dance floor, a long bar and in the distance a restaurant. There were a lot of people around.

After visiting the coat check facility, Tad led them across to the bar. It was all gleaming metal and polished wood. Glasses shimmered and the low lights reflected off racks of bottles filled with multicolored liquids. Men were spread along its length, but there was no jostling, and the bartenders, dressed in leather pants and black T-shirts, were efficient. Landry worked out that they were led by a man roughly the size of Mount Rushmore, with muscles like a Long Beach bodybuilder.

"Wow, he's huge," Landry whispered in awe.

"That's Goran," Tad said. "He's a bit of a fixture around here."

Goran must have heard his name because he made his way along the bar to serve them. "Hey, Tad, I see you've brought some new friends."

"Hi, Goran. Yes, this is Gage Roskam and his sub, Landry. They're from Seattle."

Landry felt like he was being scrutinized. Goran extended a huge paw across the bar to Gage. "Welcome to The Underground. Always a pleasure to have overseas visitors here. Am I right in thinking that there's a good club in Seattle called Scorch?"

"We're members there," Gage confirmed. "It's a pleasure to be here. The Underground is a bit of a legend within the community in the States."

"What can I get you? First drink will be on the house. After that, will you be using Mr. Ellery's tab, Tad?"

"I'll be settling the bill," Gage interrupted.

Goran nodded. "Fair enough. No alcohol if you're intending to play."

"We aren't, this time," Gage said. "But Landry will be sticking to soda, and I'll have a light beer. Tad?"

"I'll have one of those Italian fruity things you introduced me to, please, Goran."

"And me!" Landry piped up. "Please," he added after a hard look from Gage. Goran's obvious approval made him preen a little.

Goran set about getting their drinks. "It's a shame Mr. Hoffman isn't in this evening. He's the owner and he likes to meet overseas visitors personally when he can, but his partner has a few photographs in an exhibition at the Natural History Museum and there's some kind of shindig on there tonight."

"Isn't that somewhere you were going to take in, love?" Gage asked Landry.

"I was, I mean I am definitely going to go. There's a wildlife photography exhibition on."

"Alistair, Mr. Hoffman's sub, is an award-winning photographer. He had a photograph shortlisted for the urban wildlife category in the Wildlife Photographer of the Year competition."

"Oh wow, he must be amazing."

"He is. Alistair Easton, you should look him up." Goran slid their drinks across the bar. Landry's had a cute paper parasol and a cherry on a stick in it. He beamed in delight. "You'll need to come back another time because you should also definitely meet Olly. He's our resident brat. He's helping Alistair at the exhibition, though. He'd love to meet you and introduce you to his friends. You could get into all kinds of trouble."

Gage growled. "Like he needs the help."

"I think you'd get on well with Olly's Dom, Gage. Joe Dexter is a good man. He and Olly don't live in London all the time, but they have a place here. They're around a fair bit when they're not at home in Yorkshire."

"Sounds good. Okay, you two," Gage said, "Goran has other customers waiting, and we should find somewhere quiet to sit and talk."

"Best place is at the back of the restaurant area," Goran said. "You don't have to eat. Lots of people who want a bit of peace head back there."

"Thanks."

Landry appreciated Gage's protective hand on his shoulder as they strolled across the club getting curious looks from all quarters.

"I've never seen so much leather in one place," Landry whispered, taking in men of all shapes and sizes in various stages of undress. "Wow, he must be chilly." He eyed a kneeling sub wearing nothing but a butt plug tail and a collar.

Gage shook his head. "I'm sure his master is making sure he's warm. Now watch where you're going before you fall over something." He wended his way through tables to an empty one in a back corner of the restaurant. Once they were all seated, and Gage had ordered another round of drinks from an eager server, Landry looked from Tad to Gage expectantly.

"Somebody say something!"

"Patience, brat. I was about to ask Tad to take us through what's happened leading up to Ellery's disappearance. The short version if you would, Tad."

Okay, I can let my attention wander until we get to the good bit. Landry shifted to get a better view across the club and prepared to be entertained.

Chapter Twelve

While Tad brought Gage up to date, Landry took in everything going on around him, trying not to make it obvious he was watching. He loved the warm, friendly feel of The Underground that he thought the owner must have worked hard to achieve. From what he could see, the fixtures and fittings were all top quality, not the kind of place that revealed its true identity when the lights came on to expose chipped paint and stained flooring. *If someone dropped a drink in here, there'd be a sub on his knees cleaning it up in seconds.* Landry couldn't imagine a sticky surface being permitted to exist for long.

I wonder if the servers get any choice about their uniforms. The wait staff were wearing short leather kilts and that was it. An occasional sharp turn revealed a flash of underwear as skimpy as Landry was wearing. Nobody seemed unhappy about their lack of clothing and not all of them were wearing collars. *I don't think I've ever seen a more smiley bunch of servers.* Their interactions seemed respectful. No one was touching where they weren't invited.

The dance floor was packed, the music more rock than pop. There was a continual line of customers at Goran's bar and every table in the restaurant was now full. Subs knelt by their Doms or sat in their laps. One man had his partner across his knees and was giving his bare ass a firm spanking. His companions all seemed to be assisting by offering a critique of his technique. Where privacy was wanted for a discreet under-the-table blow job, eyes were averted. Where an audience was welcome, the spectators were enthusiastic and vocal.

Landry imagined Gage ordering him to his knees. *Yes, please! In here, that would be so hot.*

Tad was still talking. "So anyway, James booked a hotel for me. I moved in but haven't heard from him since. The reservation only has three days to run so whatever he was doing, he must have expected it to be over by then."

Landry paid attention now that Tad was getting to things Landry didn't yet know.

Gage frowned. "How does Ellery usually contact you went he goes on one of his trips?"

"He uses burner phones and changes them frequently. He doesn't give me the numbers—he always calls me or sends a text if he can't speak in person. This long…it makes me think he's been separated from his phone."

Landry patted Tad's knee. "Try not to worry. Ellery is sneaky and devious and… Oh, sorry…"

Tad laughed. "I know what he is, Landry, and you're not wrong."

"Even so," Gage interjected, "I think you're right to be concerned, Tad. After tomorrow, I have two days free. I think you two should stick together and carry on with your research. Find us some more leads to follow."

"Are you making me an official investigator?" Landry bounced.

"So long as you keep your head in the books and away from any gun sights. You'll be safer together." Gage drummed his fingers on his knee. "I'm wondering whether you should move from your hotel early, Tad. Is there somewhere else you could go, other than home, obviously?"

"Sure, I can crash on a mate's couch if I need to, but why?"

"Call it excessive paranoia. Ellery is a pain in my ass, but he would do anything to keep you safe. You're his weakness and if I were in his shoes, I'd have put you in that hotel to keep you safe. If there's any chance at all that someone could get to him through you, we should take further precautions."

"I'm not completely helpless."

"I'm sure but I've got a bad feeling about this, and there's no harm in being cautious. Ellery wouldn't know that Landry had been followed. If his enemies know about us, they certainly know about you."

"Trust me, I *can* take care of myself."

From his expression Gage didn't seem convinced.

"I can," Tad said with a laugh. "I'm a black belt in taekwondo, and thanks to James I'm a pretty good shot." He fiddled with a mat on the table, tearing off all four corners. "I admit, I'd prefer to have James take care of me."

Landry turned to Gage, who held up a hand. "No. You're absolutely not learning to shoot. Maybe we can check out some self-defense lessons since you're always in deep crap."

"That's not what I was going to ask," Landry protested.

"Really?"

Fuck, he can see right through me. "Okay it was, but I've already gone off the idea. I'd probably end up shooting myself."

Gage sighed. "Tad…"

"Okay! I'll go somewhere else, but only because James would say the same." Tad sagged in his seat. "I need him back."

I can't imagine what he's going through. If it were Gage who was missing, I'd be falling apart.

"Snacks. We need snacks. Food makes everything better." Landry made puppy eyes at Gage, who shrugged.

"I could eat."

"They do amazing sharing platters here," Tad said. "How about one of those?"

Gage caught the eye of a passing server and put in an order. Landry beamed.

"Don't think this is your influence, mister," Gage scolded. "Those eyes don't work on me."

Tad failed to hide a smile. "Doms see all, Landry. You should know that by now. Gage has you all worked out."

"Annoying, isn't it?"

"Oh yes."

"It's a good thing I know he likes snacks as much as I do." Landry stuck his tongue out at Tad.

"Behave. Both of you." Gage shook his head. "Can you believe some Doms have two subs? I don't see how that's possible without going insane. I have enough trouble with one."

"Hey! I'm not trouble." Landry pouted. "Well, maybe a little. Okay, a bit but I am *so* worth it."

"That's up for debate. How about we go through the clues we have so far," Gage suggested.

"Are you trying to distract me from all the hotness going on around here?" Landry eyed the St Andrews cross on the other side of the room where a Dom was flogging his naked sub.

"Yes. Focus. Unless you want to join the line to use that cross?"

"Uh, no thanks. That's more Tad's speed than mine." Landry had seen Tad take a whipping before and he'd enjoyed it. A lot.

Tad's gaze went to the cross. He ran his tongue along his lower lip and gave a happy sigh. "Feels so good."

"Pain slut."

"Slut slut."

"What does that even mean? Help me, Gage, I'm being maligned!" Landry bumped his hip against Gage's.

"You two...somebody help me." Gage was saved by the arrival of a server hefting a massive platter of food. Landry clapped his hands, delighted.

"Wowsers, that looks so good." There was a selection of cut veggies, various deep fried finger foods, miniature tartlets and puffs—it was hard to decide what to try first. Landry rescued the server by taking the tray then positioning it where they could all dip in. Landry looked at his Dom.

"Go ahead," Gage said. "I appreciate the suggestion that I might have a role here, but I'm fully aware of the danger of getting between you and snacks."

"Yum!" Landry set to with enthusiasm. "Oh, so good!"

Tad was more measured but also tucked in. Gage looked on in amused benevolence for a minute or two but then joined them. "You're right, Lan, this is all fabulous. Nice idea, Tad."

Once Landry had satisfied his initial cravings, he wiped his fingers on a napkin. "Now I can think better. Clues. Where are we at?" Gage's expression changed. "You've got that face on," Landry said.

"What face?"

"The one you get when you're detectiving. All stern and intense."

"Oh."

"It's very sexy."

"It is." Tad added his agreement.

"Good Lord." Gage gazed heavenward. "Grant me the patience not to spank both of these brats in turn."

Landry gasped and Tad gave a lazy grin in response. "James wouldn't mind. Just saying." Tad shifted in his seat, emphasizing how well black leather molded to his thighs. Landry's face heated.

"Clues," Gage said, his tone flat.

He is so thinking about it. Landry gave Gage a coy smile, aiming for subtle encouragement.

"Really, Lan?"

Landry nodded. "Ooh yeah."

"Clues first. Warming the backsides of you two reprobates later. Maybe. Not promising."

"Goody! Okay…can we all agree that the Fabergé egg is what Ellery is after? The pendant he got you to send, Tad, spelling out HELP HEN, which could have been one heck of a lot clearer I have to say, then the stained-glass window with the hens in the corner and the family crest." Lan looked from Gage to Tad. "It can't be anything else, can it?"

"He never told me explicitly, just hinted," Tad said. "But I can't think what else it could be. Something so mysterious and rare is absolutely his thing, and the letter he found would have spurred him on to do more than just desk research."

"The Ascott family's links to Russia seal it for me," Gage said. "A missing piece of the puzzle, though, is how Ellery got the picture of the window. Where is it? Is the location important? Did he go there himself or find the picture somewhere online?"

"I found the location, remember?" Landry piped up. "When I was researching the family. The house is in a village in Oxfordshire."

"Oh yeah, sorry. Brain fog caused by dancing around you two."

"He told me he'd been in Oxfordshire," Tad contributed. "That was when he called me before he came back to London for the last time. The timeline fits, so I'd say he took the picture himself. Even if he found it online initially, he would have wanted to verify it in case it had been faked. He's always really careful about verifying his leads."

"So job number one for tomorrow is for you two to try to track down the location of the window," Gage said. "I doubt the realtor's website will have an exact address, but there are plenty of ways of finding the site if you have more pictures of the property. Google Earth for one."

"And if we find it?" Landry asked. "What then?"

"See if you can identify the current owners and if they have any link to Russia, I guess. There's a possibility that Ellery went back there and got himself into trouble. If nothing else, we need to rule it out."

"You're quite good at this, aren't you?" Landry said.

"I *am* a detective, Lan. It shouldn't be that much of a surprise."

"Yeah, but you always give Sancha all the credit when you solve a case, so I have to assume she's the brains of your outfit."

Gage wrinkled his nose. "She is. Generally. But I contribute." He sounded a bit defensive. Landry patted his knee.

"Sure you do, sweetie."

"Good grief." Tad made gagging noises. "You two are Cool Whip and Marshmallow Fluff sandwiched between two double-thick Oreos."

"Are not," Gage grumbled.

"Oh, that sounds yummy!"

"No!" Gage and Tad yelled at Landry in unison.

"I'll just eat some more veggies then." Landry made sure to dip his pepper stick in the thick, creamy dip. He took his time sucking the dip off. Gage shifted in his seat and Landry grinned.

"More clues."

"Yes, Sir." Landry licked his lips real slow.

"Do you two want some privacy?" Tad asked. "'Cos there are plenty of quiet spots around the club if you need to…work off some tension."

Landry's face heated. "Sorry, Tad, I feel bad. We're supposed to be here for you. It's the atmosphere in this place. I got carried away in the moment. Forgive me?"

"You don't have a mean bone in your body, Landry, unless it's Gage's, of course." Tad smirked. "There's nothing to forgive. For fuck's sake, stop doing an impression of a baby bunny who ate the wrong carrot."

"Do I...?" Landry directed his question at Gage.

"Some." Gage tossed a leather cushion onto the floor. "Come here."

Landry sank to his knees. He leaned his chin on Gage's thigh. "Yes, Sir."

Gage tousled his hair. "We need to consider where else Ellery may have gone and also how he traveled."

"I put some thought into that," Tad said. "He always tries to stay under the radar as much as possible. He uses rental vehicles and pays cash."

"I suppose he uses a false name, too?" Gage asked.

"Yes, but I know them. We used to think them up together."

"You guys sure have a strange idea of foreplay," Landry muttered.

"Funny." Tad stuffed a smoked-salmon blini in his mouth. "He liked Ivor P. Addle, Dick Biggar, Harry Cox, Dixon Balls...you get the idea."

Landry fell about laughing and earned a glare from Gage. "What? It's funny! Juvenile, but funny."

"Fuck's sake." Gage took a long drink. "Another job for your list tomorrow. Pretend to be his PA and call up rental agencies to see if you can track down the vehicle he's in. If he's not able to get in touch for whatever reason, he may have abandoned his car. Rental companies lo-jack their vehicles."

"We could say he got drunk, got a ride home and can't remember where he left the car," Tad suggested.

Gage gave an approving nod. "Good idea. We find the car, van, whatever, chances are we get closer to finding Ellery."

Tad put his head in his hands, taking a shaky breath.

"You okay? This can't be easy."

"Not really. It's good to have a plan, though, it'll give me something to focus on. I think I'm going to head out, if you don't mind?"

"Remember, don't go back to your hotel. Send me the details, and I'll have someone drop by to get your things," Gage said.

"It might be better to leave stuff there. Make it seem like I might come back."

Gage nodded his approval. "Good thinking. I could get a foot patrol to do a walk by."

"Where shall we meet tomorrow?" Landry asked.

"I don't think I should come by your hotel again," Tad said. "There's a little internet café I know. That would be a good place to get online anonymously. I'll text the address to Gage as well as my hotel info."

"They have coffee, right?" Landry had to consider his wellbeing.

"Yes, Landry, they have coffee, cakes and computers." Tad got to his feet. "I'm sorry you got dragged into all this."

"Don't be. We're your friends. This is what friends do." Landry patted Gage's hand. "You should walk Tad to his motorcycle, love. Make sure he's safe."

"I will. Keep your knees planted on that cushion. If I come back and find you've moved, I'll borrow a riding crop, bend you over this table and let everyone here know who your Dom is."

"Sounds hot," Tad commented.

"Not moving, Sir. See ya, Tad. Be safe."

While Gage was gone, Landry developed a problematic erection thinking through various crop-related scenarios. "Should have worn looser pants." He spread his knees wider. *Still on the cushion. He didn't say I couldn't move at all. I need him to fuck me in the worst way.*

"You're fidgeting like you have ants in your pants." Gage loomed over him.

"Oh, you're back! You were gone forever."

"I was all of five minutes."

"Same difference."

"What's up?"

"Good choice of words. I am, thanks to you talking about crops."

"Ah, feeling needy, are we?" Gage pulled Landry to his feet.

"My dick hurts and my ass is twitching. Or is that my ass hurts and my dick is twitching? I don't know! You've got me all flappy." Landry wrapped his arms around Gage's waist. "Fuck me. Pleeeeease."

"You want to leave? We can go back to the hotel."

"No...I need you now." Landry didn't dare meet Gage's eyes.

"Do I have a little exhibitionist on my hands?"

"You could have him on your cock if you'd stop teasing me."

"I want to be clear, Lan. You want me to fuck you here? In public?"

"Uh-huh. Yes please, Sir."

"Jesus." Gage's burgeoning erection prodded Landry's stomach. "What's your safe word?"

"For tonight, corgi."

"You're fucking kidding me?"

"Nope."

Gage grabbed Landry's wrist then pulled him out of the dining area to a corner of the main club where a squat, padded sawhorse sat. He bent Landry over it before yanking down his pants and underwear without ceremony. "I want you looking out at all those men watching me fuck you."

Landry raised his head to find he was becoming the object of eager attention, and it turned him on even more. "Oh wow!" Gage unzipping was the best sound Landry had ever heard.

"Any royal pooches in the room?"

"No, Sir!"

"Good." Gage gave Landry's ass a firm slap. "Shit. Lube." Several packets flew through the air in their direction. Gage caught one, and seconds later his slick cock was pressed to Landry's hole. "They can't see me in you but they can see your face. They know what I'm going to do."

Landry noted several men with their hands down their pants. "Please fuck me, Sir!"

"They're watching me move. Watching me fuck you." Gage jacked his hips. "Every Dom in this room is me. Every sub is you." Gage twisted his hand into Landry's shirt, holding him in place. He drilled into him, keeping up a steady rhythm.

"Need to come so bad!" Landry groped for his cock but couldn't reach.

Gage's grunts grew louder, his thrusts harder. He ripped Landry's shirt as he came, the sounding of tearing fabric breaking through the appreciative muttering from the crowd.

"Sir, please!"

Gage flipped Landry around then dropped to his knees. He took Landry's rigid dick into his mouth, gave it a long, hard suck, and Landry came with a jubilant yell, earning them a round of applause. The gathered men drifted away, gifting them some privacy. Panting, Landry leaned against the sawhorse while Gage adjusted their clothing. "Why are you grinning?"

"I have the hottest fucking boyfriend on the planet," Gage said. "Never stop surprising me, okay?"

"I'll do my best. Did we really just do that?"

"Oh yeah." Gage scooped Landry into his arms, and Landry wrapped his legs around Gage's hips. "Now I'm taking you back to the hotel for round two. Gonna get that crop out. Leave a few marks for you to think about tomorrow."

Landry rested his head on Gage's shoulder. "Best Dom ever."

Chapter Thirteen

"This is a really cute place, Tad! I love it." Landry adored everything about the internet café, from the black-and-white movie pictures covering the walls to the jewel-colored cushions on every chair. "These cushions look like they could have come from my friend Priya's shop back in Seattle." There were several tables for people with their own laptops and a bunch of computer stations for those who didn't. Enticing aromas issued from the back of the room where a glass cabinet was stuffed with goodies.

"It's eight in the morning, how can you be this fucking cheerful?" Tad slouched in an armchair inhaling a triple espresso. "You're like the Energizer bunny on speed. You have the manic pink bunny in the States, don't you?"

"We do and I am not pink, nor a bunny. I'm high on life. Last night was amazing. I really hope we get to go back to The Underground before we go home. Gage was...inspired."

"Should I ask what you two got up to after I left?"

"I'm sure someone will tell you when you go back next time, but I'm not saying."

"Gage wouldn't ever have spanked me, would he?"

"I think he gave it serious consideration, but not without Ellery's explicit permission, no. I asked him last night. He said it wouldn't have been polite."

"Ethical Doms are no fun. Gage has big hands, I'll bet he can deliver quite a wallop."

"Are you saying Ellery would spank me if I asked him to?" Landry licked the foam off the top of his vanilla latte.

"No fucking way. He knows Gage carries a gun. He'd want to but he wouldn't. Also, I'd have his balls if he messed about with anyone else, and he knows it, though I'd make an exception for you if we were together."

"I won't tell Gage that. Let him wonder." Landry shifted in his seat trying to take the weight off the sore parts of his backside.

"You really like having your butt whipped, don't you?"

"So do you!"

"Fuck, yes. Ellery sure can handle a crop. Floggers are a bit tame. Rattan canes are fucking painful. So many delicious choices."

"When you've finished salivating about corporal punishment, do you want breakfast?"

"I haven't eaten yet, so yes." Tad handed Landry a menu. "The inside of my mate's fridge is barer than the Atacama. His couch is comfy, though."

"An empty fridge is a sad experience. I haven't eaten, either. Gage left early because he wanted to talk to some of the guys at work about Ellery's disappearance. He was gonna grab something in the cafeteria there, though they call it 'the canteen' according to Gage, which is bizarre because a canteen holds water if you're a cowboy. I believe in the whole save a horse, ride a cowboy mantra, don't you?" Landry scanned the menu. "Ooh, they have pancakes with American bacon and warm syrup. It's weird that they call it American bacon. To me it's just bacon."

"That crispy stuff is good. Do you ever stop talking?"

"I'll have that, please, with extra syrup and a hash brown and no, not if I can help it."

"Why don't you get your laptop fired up, and I'll go order," Tad said. "You want more coffee?"

"You're seriously asking *me* that question? Same again, please."

Tad eyed him. "Decaf?"

"Wash your mouth out!"

"You're too easy!"

Once they'd eaten and Landry was thoroughly caffeinated, Tad pointed him to some search engines for British property. Reverse image searching with the picture of the stained-glass window Ellery had sent Landry turned out to be a quick job. "Gage was right when he said the window would be a selling feature for a property," Landry said. "There's a whole sales history here, and I can even access the most recent realtor that dealt with the listing." He flicked through the pictures. "Here's one of the window in situ. It's definitely the right one, look at the hens and the coat of arms."

Tad leaned in for a closer look. "It says it's in the village of Barton-under-Wychwood, in Oxfordshire. James *must* have gone there."

"I wonder how he found out about the window?" Landry mused. "Something must have set him on the trail."

"It's possible he was confirming something he'd already seen. He always double and triple checks his sources when he's on the hunt for something."

"Well, the house was last purchased nine years ago. If we had an exact address, I guess it wouldn't be that difficult to find out who bought it."

"There are probably data protection issues around getting names. The land registry maybe." Tad's knee bounced. "On the bike, I could be there in under two hours. It'd be a lot easier to just go there and ask a few questions."

"Aren't you supposed to be keeping a low profile?" Landry asked.

"To hell with that. If we want to find James, we need to take action not sit around on our backsides drinking coffee."

"I like coffee. Wait, you said we."

"Of course I did. You're coming with me. If I'm getting into trouble, then so are you." Tad swallowed the last of his drink. "Besides, what kind of trouble *can* we get into in broad daylight in a rural Oxfordshire village?"

"Plenty, in my experience," Landry muttered. "But that shouldn't stop us."

"If I don't do something, I'm going to curl up in a ball and cry. I can't do that. Maybe after I have James back, but not right now."

"Aw, Tad, I'm sorry. This isn't easy, is it?"

"No. It helps having you to talk to, though. I'm not usually this…chatty."

"Prefer the strong, silent vibe, huh?"

"Can we go now?"

"I can't believe I'm the one being the voice of caution," Landry said, "but there's another thing we should try to do first. If Ellery did find trouble in Oxfordshire, shouldn't we see if we can get a location for his missing rental?"

"That's actually a good idea," Tad said.

"Hey! I have brilliant ideas all the time."

"Of course you do."

Landry pursed his lips. "How are we going to do this?"

"James always used bigger rental companies and there aren't many of those. If we both make calls pretending to be his PA, we just have to persuade the customer service people to give up the information."

"Wouldn't it be better if we pretended to be him?" Landry suggested.

"Well, I might be able to pull that off, but I don't think you could, unless you can do an English accent. How about we try both. We'll have to use his pseudonyms so we might need to make several calls using different combinations."

"Won't these companies get suspicious?"

"I guess they use call centers, probably in India. It's unlikely we'd speak to the same person twice, and they'll want to get paid any excess charges for the car. Probably get bonuses for resolving queries quickly too, so I doubt they'll be that bothered. It might be easier than we think."

Landry had a pad and pen so, after a bit of searching, Tad wrote a list of car rental companies then made a grid using Ellery's pseudonyms. "We'll start with these two because I know they're the ones he was using most recently. I'll start at the top of the list, and you work up from the bottom."

"Okay. This is gonna be fun." To avoid being heard on each other's calls, they moved to separate tables as far apart as they could manage.

In the end, it was Landry that got lucky. His desperate act as Harry Cox's beleaguered personal assistant trying not to get fired by locating his drunk of a boss' missing car hit home. He had the customer service lady commiserating about terrible bosses and the evils of drink before she handed over GPS coordinates for the car, a gray Toyota.

"Score!" Landry's yell as he waved his cell in Tad's direction made him the center of attention for the rest of the café's bemused patrons. "Gitika in Kolkata is a sweetheart."

"Don't worry about him," Tad said to no one in particular as he strolled over. "He's an American." There were a lot of understanding, sympathetic noises, and people went back to their conversations and computers. Tad hooked his arm through Landry's then hauled him off the premises.

"I should get an Oscar!" Landry exclaimed.

"Yeah, yeah. You were lucky."

"I was brilliant. And I made a friend in India. Where do we go first, house or car?"

"Which is closest?"

"Don't know. Slow down and I'll have a look." Landry pulled up the maps app on his cell and checked out both locations. "They're not that far apart, maybe thirty miles, but the house is closer."

"Okay, my bike is a couple streets away behind a mate's tattoo place. I brought a spare jacket and helmet in case we needed them."

"Yay! I always wanted to be a biker." Landry said, not bothering to hide the sarcasm. He trotted to keep up with Tad's longer stride.

"What the fuck am I doing?" Tad muttered. "This has disaster written all over it. Hold on tight, don't throw up over me and don't fall off. I wouldn't want to explain to Gage why he had to come get you from Accident and Emergency."

"You'd end up in there, too."

"Exactly."

Two hours later, Landry had decided his ass wasn't experienced enough for long distance motor biking, especially not after a recent paddling. Tad had pulled up outside the gates to the house in Barton-under-Wychwood, and Landry half climbed, half fell off the pillion seat.

"That seat needs a *lot* more padding," he complained, rubbed his aching backside.

Tad, graceful as a ballet dancer, swung his leg across the seat. "You get used to it." He put the kickstand down. "The bike should be fine here, it's the back end of nowhere, not crime central."

"So, what do we do now?" Landry asked. "Just walk up to the front door?"

"Why not? I think you should play a hapless American tourist looking for your hotel after getting lost on a hike. You don't have your phone, and this was the first house you came to."

"You think that's gonna work?" Landry was dubious.

"You have any better ideas? You had two hours getting here to think of something."

"I was too busy hanging on for dear life. What's the speed limit in this country anyway?"

Tad grinned. "I got you here in one piece, didn't I?"

"Fine, though my ass doesn't agree. How bad can it be? I guess the homeowner just shuts the door in my face if they're not feeling charitable."

"We don't tend to shoot people on the doorstep over here."

"Good to know!"

"I'll wait here. I'll give you, say, thirty minutes and if you're not back I'll come and find you. We need to dirty you up a bit first, though." Tad pointed at a muddy puddle. "Jump up and down in that. You need to look like you've been walking cross country for hours." He scooped up some muck then smeared it across Landry's cheek.

"Hey, stop that!" Landry stomped around in the puddle until his shoes were coated and the bottom of his jeans had turned brown and soggy. "This isn't the fun adventure I thought it was going to be."

Tad added a few smears of mud to Landry's hair, messing it up with his fingers. "Much better. Just put on that sweet innocent act you do so well, and you'll be fine."

"I *am* sweet and innocent. I'm going right off you. If I get dead, I'm telling Gage it's your fault."

"Pretty sure I can convince him this was your idea." Tad picked a juicy stem of grass and started chewing on the end of it, looking for all the world like he'd taken a break from a leisurely ride.

"I hate you." Landry shook a clod of mud from his foot.

"You love me. I'm very lovable."

Muttering under his breath, Landry stomped across the lane, pushed open the gate then made his way up the drive to the front door of the property. He turned to check and confirmed that neither the road, nor Tad, were visible from the house. There were two expensive cars parked in the turning circle out front. He was about to ring the bell when the door swung open.

"Saw you on the security camera. Can I help you?" The man who opened the door was a bit of a silver fox.

"I hope so." Landry launched into his pitiful tale, throwing in a few sniffles to enhance his performance. "So, do you have a phone I could use? Then I'll be out of your hair." He swayed.

"You're dead on your feet. Come in and I'll fetch my mobile."

"I can wait here," Landry said. He gestured at his feet, "I don't want to get your hall rug all dirty."

"Kick off your shoes. Dirt can be cleaned up."

"Okay...if you're sure." Landry toed off his footwear then padded into the hall, gazing around with open curiosity. "You have a great place here. Everything in this country is so old. Oh, sorry, that wasn't meant to be rude. I love it, all the old stuff, you know."

"If you need the bathroom while I find my phone, it's top of the stairs on the left."

"I'm good." Landry didn't want to sound too eager.

"You have mud on your face and in your hair."

"Oh! Geez, I must look like a hobo. Top of the stairs, right?"

"Go ahead."

Landry went straight to the bathroom and did a half decent job of undoing Tad's special effects to make himself respectable. He used the toilet, washed his hands then made his way down the stairs, stopping to admire the stained-glass window he was already so familiar with. He arrived at the bottom of the stairs at the same time as his host.

"That window is unbelievable. Is it Tiffany?"

"Not an original, I'm sad to say. But it did sell the house to me. The family that had it built originally put the window in. It's a copy of a Tiffany window but they added some family related touches of their own."

"The crest isn't yours, then? That would be so cool, to have a family crest."

"No, the crest belongs to the Ascott family, but I don't know anything about them. Here, make your call."

Landry called Tad. He repeated his story including a few compliments for his host. "No, I don't know where I am, I'm lost. How would I know that?" He poked his tongue out at the phone. "Would you mind explaining to my friend where we are, Mr...."

"Call me Roger." He took the phone back and gave a detailed explanation of the location and how to find the house. He listened to whatever Tad was saying then disconnected. "That's good, your friend isn't that far away. He says he'll be here in about ten minutes, maybe fifteen. In the meantime, can I offer you a cup of tea?"

"I don't want to put you out. You've already been so kind."

"You won't be. I was about to make a pot anyway. I work from home and I have to force myself to take breaks otherwise I'd go a bit crazy. Come through to the kitchen. You can tell me all about yourself."

Within five minutes, Landry found himself sitting at a kitchen table sipping from a mug of hot tea with a slice of Victoria sponge on a plate at his elbow. Not seeing any need to dissemble, he'd told Roger about the store in Seattle and why he was in England with Gage.

Roger in turn had given up a few details about his work as an architect and his love of ornithology. Landry had quickly come to the conclusion that Roger had nothing to do with whatever mystery Ellery was tied up with. He just happened to live in a property that was connected. By the time Tad arrived, Landry and Roger were gossiping like old mates and Landry was reluctant to leave.

"Thank you so much for your hospitality," he said. "This day turned out so much better than I thought it was going to." He put on his dirty shoes in the porch where Tad handed over his jacket and helmet.

"I can't leave you alone for five minutes, can I? I told you not to go wandering off on your own," Tad scolded. "I'm sorry to put you to so much trouble," he said to Roger.

"It was no trouble. A welcome interlude in a busy day. Feel free to come back for a visit if you find yourself at a loose end again, Landry. I'd like to hear more about life in Seattle and bird life in the Pacific northwest. Bring your partner, too."

"That's so kind. I will." Landry mounted the bike behind Tad and waved at his new friend as they drove away. Tad rode to the next village before pulling over in the car park of a pub called the Fox and Badger.

"Let's get lunch and a drink here, and you can tell me how you managed to become lifelong buddies with a complete stranger in less than fifteen minutes."

"Lunch sounds great. I want one of those meals in a basket I've read about," Landry said.

"This isn't the 1970s, you're more likely to get gourmet haute cuisine in a pub nowadays. Inside."

"Are you mad at me?" Landry trailed after him as Tad went into the ancient building.

"No. Just realizing why you need a Dom. Gage really does have his hands full with you."

"I'm sure I have no idea what you mean. Feed me. I'm much easier to handle when I have a full belly."

Chapter Fourteen

James Ellery stamped up and down his prison cell in a vain attempt to get warm. The outbuilding next to the Russian's farmhouse might once have provided storage for vegetables or animal feed, but now it was bare. The rough-hewn stone absorbed the light, leaving behind an oppressive gloom. The only source of illumination was a single bare bulb dangling from the ceiling. When illuminated, it cast a dim, eerie spotlight which Ellery avoided as he walked.

The days were blending into a monotonous cycle, and if it hadn't been for the scratches he made on the walls, like the Count of Monte Cristo, Ellery would have lost track of how long he'd been in the outbuilding. He scratched his chin, annoyed at the rough beard that had grown. The air in his prison was thick and musty, laden with the stench of rotting wood. The only sound was the rhythmic drip of water from the roof, he guessed from a cracked tile. There was no window, and the walls were so thick there was no chance of hearing noise from outside or of anyone hearing him if he shouted for help, for that matter. Since he'd been summarily thrown into the room, he'd had no contact with Anatoly Volkov. He'd been provided with basic food, water and a bucket which was changed daily. Other than that, he'd had no human contact.

What I wouldn't give for a hotel bathroom right now. And who the fuck grows a beard voluntarily, this itches like the devil?

For Ellery, boredom was the worst kind of torture. He didn't spare a thought for what Volkov might do to him but spent his time worrying about Tad and whether or not he was okay. It had been much longer than usual that Ellery had been out of touch. "You'll be worrying. Talk to Gage Roskam, Tad. He'll know what to do." Talking to himself really didn't help.

Ellery sat against the wall for a while, but the damp seeped through his shirt, chilling his skin. The cold stone floor made his ass ache. *I wonder if this is how Tad feels after a spanking.* His jacket had been taken but he was grateful he hadn't been stripped naked. *This could be a lot worse.* He judged the time by the meals he was brought and guessed that it must be almost dinner time. He was rewarded by the stomp of booted feet outside and the creak of the door.

"Boss wants to talk to you." In the gloom, Ellery couldn't make out the speaker's face, but he didn't care. He wanted out of the storeroom regardless of whether or not his destination was a worse option.

"Then lead the way, I'd hate to keep him waiting considering how…obliging he's been."

"Not so fast, genius." Ellery was pushed against the wall and his wrists cuffed behind his back. "Now we can go, and watch your mouth."

Ellery stumbled over the doorstep, cursing as he banged his knee on the frame. It was raining in the yard, and it all looked similarly depressing as to when he'd first arrived. He blinked, his eyes watering at the daylight after the gloom of his prison. He was shoved across the yard then into the kitchen where he had been prepping food a few days earlier. Then he was manhandled through the house to Volkov's study before being pushed to his knees.

The Russian, seated behind his desk, turned in his swivel chair then got to his feet.

He's doing a fine impression of a Bond villain. All he needs is a cat.

"Hello again, Mr. Ellery, I hope your accommodations have been…uncomfortable."

If he lets out a manic cackle, I'm going to laugh, I won't be able to help myself. Ellery pressed his lips together in a tight line.

Volkov was wearing a black suit, white shirt and a deep red tie that to Ellery's tired eyes resembled a slash of blood down his chest.

"Adequate. I won't be giving the place any five-star reviews on TripAdvisor."

"Do you really think in your position, sarcasm is appropriate?"

"What do you want me to do, cry?"

"I would enjoy that, some begging perhaps, screaming also works, but maybe later." Volkov picked up a piece of paper from his desk then held it up so that Ellery could see it. There was a rudimentary sketch on it of what Ellery assumed was supposed to be the hen with a sapphire pendant egg.

"Do you recognize this?"

"It's a jeweled Fabergé egg," Ellery said. It wasn't worth lying about.

"Where is it?"

"I was hoping you could tell me that."

Volkov backhanded Ellery across the face, knocking him down. Volkov's goons put Ellery back on his knees. He probed at the split in his lip with his tongue, tasting copper.

"Shall we try that again?" Volkov flexed his hands as if he had hurt his knuckles. Several of them cracked.

"Could you not do that, gives me the willies? I've no idea where it is and you hitting me isn't going to change anything."

"You expect me to believe you?"

"Not at all. You don't seem like the trusting type, but why do you think I came here? If I knew where the egg was I'd have it, wouldn't I?"

"Unfortunately for you, that does make sense. We found the bugs that you planted, of course. But I don't believe that you have no useful information. It would be in your best interest to tell me what you've uncovered so far."

"And why would I do that?"

Volkov hit him again. "To avoid causing yourself significant pain. I'll give you twenty-four hours to consider your position. This time tomorrow we'll discuss what you know in more detail. Take him away and hose him down, he stinks."

The Russian's goons took Volkov literally. They dragged Ellery out into the yard and washed him down using a garden hose before hauling him back to the storage shed. They did remove the handcuffs before leaving him soaked and shivering in the darkness. The light was off and the switch for it wasn't in the room. It didn't escape Ellery's notice that a meal was not forthcoming.

"Well, fuck. This situation just gets better and better." He sat against the wall once more, arms wrapped around his knees and wondered what would get him first, hypothermia or the Russian.

* * * *

"I can't believe that pub did scampi and chips in a basket," Tad grumbled as he and Landry ambled out of the pub to the car park. "It was like stepping back in time in there. The cheese plowman's *was* good, though."

"I can cross that one off my bucket list," Landry said. "It was yummy, too."

"Aren't you a bit young to have one of those? Or is it because you get into so many scrapes your life expectancy is reduced?"

"Funny. You should talk to your boyfriend about that. My list of stuff I wanna try keeps growing so I figure it's never too soon to start. You should definitely have one. I've recently added magnet fishing and mudlarking."

Tad rammed his helmet on his head. "I'll give it due consideration. Where are we going next?"

Landry checked his cell for the coordinates that the rental car lady had given him. "Uh oh, I have three missed calls from Gage. I turned the ringer down and forgot to reset it. I'd better call him or half the cops in England will be descending on us." He took a few steps away from Tad then made the call. "Hi, honey, sorry I missed your calls."

"Landry Benjamin Carran, I am going to lock you in a dungeon and throw away the key. What the ever-loving fuck are you doing in Oxfordshire when you should be in London?"

"How do you...? Oh, I forgot you have a tracker on my phone."

"No shit. Landry, I swear you're going to put me in an early grave. Where are you exactly?"

"You don't need to worry. I'm with Tad. We've been tracking down the house with the stained-glass window and now we're going to retrieve Ellery's rental car. I got the coordinates out of the rental company by pretending to be his PA." There was a lot of spluttering at the other end of the line. "Gage? Are you okay? Are you choking on something because somebody should give you the Heimlich maneuver?"

"Do you recall me explicitly telling you not to do anything dangerous?" Gage's voice was far too quiet. Landry swallowed.

"Yes, Sir."

"And do you think that disappearing halfway across the country without telling me where you're going, presumably on the back of Tad's motorcycle, isn't dangerous?"

"Oh no, it's really pretty around here. Everyone is very nice. The guy that owns the house gave me tea and cake. Tad and I also had a great lunch in this quaint old pub and... That's not what you wanted to hear, is it?"

"I... He... You are unbelievable. Get your ass back here to London right now."

"I'm kinda reliant on Tad for a ride, and he's not gonna want to come back without finding the rental first." There was an ominous silence. "Gage, are you there?"

When Gage spoke, Landry knew it was through gritted teeth. "When you find the car, call me. I'll arrange for local law enforcement to pick it up. Then no more detours. I want you in our hotel room when I get back from work. Then you and I are going to have a conversation."

"Yes, Sir."

"Promise me, Landry. Right back here."

"Right back. I promise. To be fair, my backside doesn't want to spend any more time on Tad's bike than is strictly necessary. His suspension is kinda hard."

"A sore ass is the least of your worries," Gage said.

Despite the implied threat, Landry's cock hardened. "Are you going to punish me, Sir?"

"Yes, Landry I'd say that's an absolute certainty." Gage disconnected, and Landry hobbled across to the bike.

"We are in big trouble. I forgot Gage had a tracker on my cell."

"There's no we involved here. You're in trouble, I'm not." Tad straddled the bike.

"But when we find Ellery, and we will find him, Gage is gonna tell him everything. He's going to say you led me astray."

"Oh shit."

Landry clambered onto the pillion seat. "Yeah, that."

With satnav coordinates it didn't take them long to find Ellery's abandoned rental car, even though Tad almost missed it. It was Landry who spotted the end of the vehicle sticking out from behind a bush. Ellery had pulled off the road and left the car tucked behind a stand of trees.

Landry and Tad dismounted and took off their helmets. "What on earth was he doing here?" Tad asked. "There's nothing here."

"I guess we need to look on a map," Landry said. "He may have gone somewhere on foot. How are you at breaking into vehicles?"

"No need. If he walked somewhere he would have left the key. Try under the wheel arch on the far side of the car."

"Got it!" Landry found the key sitting on top of the tire. "You think maybe we shouldn't touch anything?"

Tad shrugged. "There's no sign here that he didn't leave the car voluntarily. Whatever happened to him, I don't think it happened here. You should be safe to take a look inside."

"Okay." Landry took the passenger side while Tad got in behind the wheel. "I don't get it."

"What?"

"What kind of a rental is this? Where are the candy wrappers and soda cans?"

"This isn't your car, Landry. Check the glove compartment."

"Gage keeps his gun in his. Oh, there's a cell." Landry jabbed the phone several times, but the screen stayed black. "Battery is dead, though. Nothing else apart from some paperwork from the rental company."

Tad turned on the ignition. "Assuming it was set to zero from point of rental, there's nothing unusual about the mileage." He sighed. "I'm not sure what I expected to find."

"I'll call Gage," Landry said, "let him know we found the car and Ellery's cell. I think we should get back to London. I'd quite like to limit the amount of trouble I'm in."

"Okay. We can charge the mobile when we get back and see if there's anything interesting on it."

"And research the area. See if we can work out why Ellery was here."

Landry checked in with Gage and, once he'd listened to another scolding, relayed the latest information.

"He says we both need to get our asses back to London, stat. But I also have to tell you not to speed. That's kind of contradictory, but that's Gage."

Tad grinned. "By tonight I think you're going to have fond memories of being a little saddle sore. Let's go."

Back in London, Tad left his bike in a Soho backstreet then he and Landry made their way to Landry's hotel by separate routes. Landry's favorite doorman was nowhere to be seen but the reception area was empty. *Guess Winston has been dealing with Fedora Man, like he promised.*

When Tad arrived they headed up to Landry's room. He ordered a pot of coffee and donuts from room service while Tad plugged Ellery's cellphone in to charge.

"When the food arrives, don't touch the custard donut," Landry said. "It's Gage's favorite and he'll be here in a few minutes. He sent me a text saying he was on his way."

"I'm not sure one donut is going to soften his spanking hand," Tad said.

"It has to be worth a try, though, right?" Landry changed his pants for a pair that were less mud-spattered, leaving his shoes in the bathroom to clean later. "Plus, we get treats, too. And I need coffee in the worst way."

"How the hell do you stay so slim? It's not that long since we had lunch." Tad lounged in a chair.

"Fast metabolism. I grew up with older twin brothers and I learned to move fast to get the best snacks. Survival of the fittest. I put it down to that."

"I'm not sure that's how it works, Landry."

"You're not going to get all scientific on me, are you? Donuts and coffee are survival tactics, go with it."

Room service arrived at the same time as Gage, who tipped the porter then carried the tray into the room. He put it on a low table before looking from Tad to Landry. "You two are a massive pain in my ass, you know that?"

Landry gave him his sweetest smile. "I missed you. I love you. I'm sorry, Sir."

"I'm not," Tad said.

"Not helping, Tad." Landry scowled at him.

"At least he's honest. You're only sorry you got caught, Landry. We'll discuss your misbehavior later. I arranged for the rental car to be retrieved. Where's the cell you found?"

"Charging," Landry said. "We wanted to wait for you before we took a look at it."

"Miracles happen." Gage grabbed the custard donut. "Pour some coffee, Lan, I get the feeling it's going to be a long evening and this" — he took a bite of the donut — "is not enough to save you from punishment."

Once the charge level of Ellery's cell had climbed out of single digits, Gage took a hold of it.

"There's a four-digit pass code. Tad, you know what it is?"

"Try six-nine-six-nine."

"Of course. Why would it be anything else?" Gage tapped in the numbers. "I'm in. Unbelievable." He scrolled through the apps. "Not much on here. Seems he was careful to delete anything outgoing. There's nothing in the email inbox, no text messages. There's a non-standard app here, though. Looks like this phone was linked to some kind of listening device. Let's hope it recorded something before the battery went dead."

Tad sat forward in his chair and Landry bounced. "This is so exciting!"

"I'm not familiar with this software... Here we go." Gage pressed play.

There was a clink of china and the confusing sound of several conversations going on at the same time.

"Coffee, Sir?"

"That's James," Tad exclaimed.

"Sounds like he was waiting at a party or something," Landry said. After a few moments, the conversation muted and a single, accented voice took over. "Watch your words, gentlemen. Our server is not what he seems. He has an interest in the item we're here to discuss, and I would hazard a guess that there's a bug in this room." There was the general sound of movement.

"They're searching for the bug," Gage said. The recording went dead. "And they found it."

"Whoever was speaking, he recognized James," Tad said. "James couldn't have been expecting that."

"There's another recording file," Gage said, "but it's empty. He must've planted a second bug and they found that, too. They knew what they were doing. The man in charge, his accent sounded Russian to me."

"That's a clue, right?" Landry asked, his anxiety growing. Tad's face was bone white, and he looked like he might throw up at any moment.

"There are several leads here," Gage said. "But it's not something we should be tackling alone. I'm going to call a British colleague then head back to the station. You two are to stay here." He held up a hand, silencing Tad's protests. "I mean it. I can't be worrying about what you two are up to while I'm dealing with this. We need to move fast, so don't argue with me."

"Please find him, Sir," Landry whispered.

"I should have started looking sooner," Tad muttered.

"You weren't to know. Ellery has form. None of this is your fault, Tad." Gage sounded reassuring but Landry detected worry lines around his eyes.

"Go detect!" He nibbled on a fingernail. "Call me as soon as you know anything."

"I will." Gage took the time to give Landry a bruising kiss then he was gone.

Chapter Fifteen

Time passed, but Ellery had no concept of how long. The cold sank into his bones. He had stopped shivering a while back, but he didn't know if that was good or bad. The warmth of the Russian's study was an enticing prospect even if it came with a downside. When the storeroom door finally opened, Ellery was relieved. He didn't need to spend any more time alone with his own thoughts.

This time it was Anatoly Volkov himself who arrived, accompanied by two of his thugs. One of them pointed a gun at Ellery's head while the other chained his wrists before hauling him to his feet. The length of chain was just long enough to reach a hook in one of the ceiling beams. Someone turned on the light, the bare bulb painful to Ellery's eyes.

"Do you know the symptoms of hypothermia, Mr. Ellery?" The Russian had a relaxed stance, feet apart, hands clasped behind his back. His attire had changed like he'd dressed for the occasion. The suit was gone, replaced by dark gray cargo pants and a black sweatshirt.

Ellery didn't bother to answer. *Let him talk. The longer he takes the better.*

"Not feeling talkative? Well, I'll educate you. Mild hypothermia causes shivering, confusion and slurred speech. As it progresses your breathing will slow and get shallow. Your pulse will weaken, and you'll lose coordination. Your judgment will be impaired, though I think by coming here, that point has already been proved, don't you?"

Ellery couldn't keep his feet flat on the floor without the chains cutting into his flesh. He balanced on his toes, aware that he wouldn't be able to maintain the stance for long.

"Eventually you will lose consciousness. But that would be too easy. I enjoy conversation and I think you are a somewhat intelligent man. I think we should discuss Fabergé and his missing treasures, don't you?"

"I already told you I don't know where the egg is."

"But you have ideas about where it might be hidden, don't you? I've been tracking your progress ever since the new rumors about its existence surfaced. That was around the time you located a certain ruby bracelet. Enlisting your American friends was a clever touch."

Fuck. Now I have to worry about Gage and Landry as well as Tad. Maybe not, Gage is too fucking stubborn to die, and he'd burn down the world before he let anyone hurt Landry.

"I've been keeping my eye on them, too. The blond is cute. I'd enjoy spending some time with him. Your pretty boyfriend comes across as a bit too headstrong. I prefer my men subservient. My women too, for that matter."

Ellery didn't rise to the bait, though his hopes of getting out of his current predicament were fading fast. He didn't want to give headspace to Volkov's bedroom proclivities.

"I think you came here hoping for a shortcut. That I might give away the egg's location. Perhaps you thought I'd already obtained it and you planned to take it from me because I know you are a skilled thief. The bracelet you tracked down had been stolen to order for me. Was that where you got your lead on the egg?"

"I think you already know it was."

"I wasn't certain, but that bracelet was originally purchased by Frederick Ascott for his lover. He meant to give it to her when she arrived in England, but she never did."

"So where do *you* think the egg is?"

"I'm sorry to disappoint you but it wasn't where I expected it to be. I've put a lot of time, effort and money into tracking it down. It rightfully belongs in Russian hands, don't you think? My investors do."

"There we'll have to disagree," Ellery said, thankful that his words were not yet slurred. He was already losing the feeling in his arms. The Ascott connection was fascinating and at least he now knew why Volkov had been onto him. Volkov was uncomfortably close to the truth about the reason for Ellery's visit. He wouldn't hold back in trying to find out more. "You have no more right to the egg than anyone else."

"Finders keepers, I think you say."

"Exactly."

"Lev here used to work in a circus, you know." Volkov gestured at one of his men.

"Enthralling. As a clown, I assume."

Lev's scowl gave Ellery a brief moment of satisfaction.

"He joined as a young boy but saw working for me as a better prospect for his career. He wasn't a clown. Would you like to know what his act was?"

"Freak show?" After a nod from Volkov, Lev rewarded that comment with several punches to Ellery's ribs. Ellery swung in his chains, fighting to regain his balance. "Some people have no sense of humor." He coughed, groaning at the pain.

"Lev spent many years mastering the art of the bullwhip. He could whip an apple off the top of a pretty girl's head or slice a candle in two."

Oh fuck. Only then did Ellery notice the whip coiled against Lev's hip.

"Cut off his shirt." Volkov took a few paces back while his second goon slashed at Ellery's shirt with a pocketknife, ripping the fabric away in strips. "Your skin is cold so you won't feel much at first, but the pain will build in a most gratifying way, I can assure you."

"Aren't you going to ask me what I know?"

"Oh, we're past that point Mr. Ellery. Not that I think you have any intention of telling me anything useful. Even if you did, you are a thorn in my side. I will enjoy listening to you scream. We'll get to the questions soon enough."

The whip cracked through the air like a pistol shot. A line of fire blossomed across Ellery's shoulders and despite his resolution not to give Volkov the satisfaction, Ellery moaned. *It's not the first time you've taken a whipping, Ellery. Man up.* The second strike elicited a whimper through his gritted teeth. *Training to be an empathetic Dom was somewhat different. Fuck me, that hurts.* He screamed when the third blow landed. Volkov's grin was short-lived, however, when another of his men crashed through the door.

"Had a call from your boy in blue. Pigs are on the way. We have an hour, two at most, before they get here."

Volkov pursed his lips. "What a shame. I was beginning to enjoy myself, but it seems my entertainment is to be interrupted. Mr. Ellery, your luck will run out sooner or later. Another time." Volkov turned away. "Leave him. Dealing with him will slow the police down when they get here. Get everyone on the road north. Send word to prep the jet. There's nothing here for them to find apart from our guest and all the cow-shit they'll have to wade through. Small wins."

In minutes, Ellery was left alone. *I don't feel lucky. Two hours. Just have to last two hours.* In his head, he retreated to a well-appointed dungeon alone with Tad. He imagined every scenario he'd ever dreamed about. Role play, predicament bondage, chastity play, edging... He had an endless supply of dreams to keep his mind off the pain and brutal cold.

He was barely conscious when the storeroom door banged open. Several people crowded into the space.

"He's here!"

Ellery laughed and found he couldn't stop until the laughter turned to tears of relief.

"Ellery, you bastard. If you're not dead, I'm gonna kill you." He was held in strong arms while the chain holding him up was lifted from its hook.

"Gage?" Ellery sagged, his shoulders and arms on fire as his circulation returned. "Took you long enough."

"Fucking ingrate. Anything broken?"

Ellery shook his head. "Woah!" His world tilted as Gage put him into a fireman's carry before hauling him across the yard to the house. *I'm never going to live this down.*

Gage dumped him on Volkov's cream couch. It gave Ellery a small measure of satisfaction to think how difficult it would be to get the bloodstains out. *Not that he's ever likely to come back here.* "Anatoly Volkov. He knows about Tad and Landry. I need to get to them."

"Stay the fuck down," Gage snapped. "They're safe. As soon as the Met guys connected the dots and realized Volkov was involved in this shit show, they had armed men patrolling outside our hotel in less than twenty minutes. Landry and Tad are there together. If they try to leave, I've told the guys to Taser their disobedient asses."

"Okay. That's good."

"Let the medic do his thing."

Gage backed off while a young paramedic with blue hair assessed Ellery's condition, turning him carefully to examine his back. "He's extremely cold, and we're a long way from the nearest hospital. I'm a biker paramedic, Mr. Ellery, there's no ambulance here yet, though it shouldn't be long." He turned to Gage. "If we can warm him up here, we should. Get blankets, towels, any bedding. If there's a bath, fill it with warm water. Not too hot, we'll need to increase his temperature gradually."

Ellery drifted in and out of awareness while first aid was administered. Around him, men were searching the property. "They won't find anything," he muttered. "Volkov's gone. Said he was going north, but that could be misdirection. He was informed you were coming. Has a spy in the camp. A cop."

Gage dumped a pile of blankets on top of him. "Wonderful. This shit show gets better and better."

"Bath's ready," someone yelled.

"Guess the local cops are okay with us using the facilities," Gage said.

"He needs getting out of what's left of his clothes," the medic contributed. "They're cold, wet and filthy. I need to know if he has more injuries."

"You do it." Ellery said to Gage. "Just you."

"That okay with you?" Gage asked the medic.

"Sure, whatever gets this done. I'll wait outside the bathroom. Yell if you need me. None of his injuries are going to kill him but hypothermia might."

Ellery was shaking uncontrollably now his temperature had edged away from Arctic, his teeth chattering so hard he couldn't get any more words out. He was grateful Gage was strong enough to lift him because he wasn't walking anywhere.

In the bathroom, Gage sat him on the toilet. "Can you undress yourself?"

Ellery couldn't even manage the button on his pants. "Nnnno."

"You ever, and I mean *ever*, talk to anyone about this, I will hunt you down." Gage stripped him quickly then lifted him into the bath. The water felt scalding, and Ellery flailed. "That's fucking hot! Are you trying to boil me alive?"

"It's barely warm. Stop struggling. Fuck it." Gage rolled up his pant legs then stepped into the bath. He stood to either side of Ellery's hips, bracing him, then ladled warm water over his body. The water turned pinky brown.

"Everything okay in there?" the medic yelled from outside the door.

"There is nothing okay about this situation," Gage mumbled. "All good! Increasing the water temperature now."

"You always wanted to get me naked," Ellery said. His teeth had stopped banging together, and he no longer felt like he was lying in acid.

"Fuck-all wrong with your mouth, is there?" Gage clambered out of the tub. "You have an impressive amount of bruises. You might want to avoid getting beaten up and whipped in future."

"Really? I was thinking of repeating the experience next week. How did you find me?"

Gage added more hot water to the tub. "Landry and Tad. Your boy needs an epic spanking, by the way."

"He usually does."

"They teamed up, God help us, tracked down your rental vehicle. A quick look into properties in the area brought up a giant red flag. A red, white and blue one actually, and I'm not talking about the Union Jack. It wasn't much of a stretch to connect Russian treasure with a Russian gangster." Gage ladled hot water over Ellery's body. "What the fuck did you think you were doing, coming here alone? From what I've been told, Volkov is ruthless. He's suspected of multiple killings."

"You can add the Ascott family to that list."

"Way ahead of you. Well, Landry is. He already asked me to look into the deaths of the father and the son."

"Clever boy."

"Yes, he is. Sometimes I wish he wasn't quite so bright, though his common sense is somewhat lacking, as is his sense of self-preservation. I can't believe you got him involved with your fucking treasure hunts yet again."

"He loves me. I'm adorable. Also, I feel a lot better, so how about you find me a towel, unless you want more time alone with my spectacular bod."

"Fuck's sake. Drowning you seems a better option." There was a robe hanging on the back of the bathroom door, so Gage grabbed it.

"Can you give me a hand, still a bit weak?" Gage hauled Ellery upright then thrust the robe at him. "Don't fancy giving me a nice rubdown then?"

"I'm leaving you to the tender mercies of that paramedic. He's young, so try not to psychologically scar him for life." Gage flung open the door then ushered the medic in. "If you could come up with some really uncomfortable procedures for him, I'd very much appreciate that."

"I'm not going to a hospital," Ellery said. "Patch me up. Detective Roskam will be looking after me."

The medic gave Gage questioning glance. Gage growled and the young man took a couple steps back.

"And could someone maybe find me some clothes?"

"I suppose I'm better off keeping him where I can see him," Gage grumbled. "Let me know when he's fit to travel. I have some calls to make. Don't take any crap from him." He grabbed his boots and socks then gave his feet a cursory rub with a towel before putting them on.

"Don't worry, sweetheart, I'm a big pussycat. How do you feel about handcuffs?" Ellery said, loud enough for Gage to catch as he headed back down the stairs.

"Don't commit murder on foreign soil. Don't commit murder on foreign soil. Perhaps if I say it often enough it'll will stop me. I like the Brits, but they don't need another homicide to deal with." After letting his colleagues know that Ellery was going to be okay and that they'd need a ride back to London, Gage went outside for some fresh air. He took a calming breath then called Landry.

"Gage! What's going on? You are so bad at keeping in touch."

"Sorry, love. Things got busy fast. We've got Ellery and he's fine."

"Tad! Gage has found James and he's okay." Landry yelled so loud that Gage had to hold his cell away from his ear. "That's amazing news. Where are you?"

"Oxfordshire. I'll explain everything when we get back. It'll probably be a while because the Brits will want to take Ellery's statement before they let him go."

"Okay, should I bring Tad to the police station?"

"No, stay put. See if you can book a room for them at our hotel would you?"

"I can do that, though if we had a slumber party it would be more fun."

"Landry, even if the world were ending, if nuclear Armageddon was on the horizon, nothing could induce me to spend the night in the same room as James Ellery."

"Seems a tad extreme, Sir, but okay. Let me know when you leave the cop shop. Will Ellery be able to call Tad, because he's bouncing around the room like a spaniel on steroids?"

"As soon as the medic has finished with him."

"Wait, what?" Landry yelled, "You didn't say anything about him being hurt."

"Well shit, I didn't mean to let that slip out. He's walking wounded, he's going to be fine. Please let Tad know that he hasn't lost any vital body parts. Sadly, his mouth is working just fine."

"Good to know."

"I need to go, Lan. I'll see you in a few hours." Big, smoochy kissing noises ended the call. "That's if I can survive two hours in a car with the Brit from hell without getting myself arrested for assault and battery."

* * * *

It was almost midnight by the time Gage and Ellery got back to the hotel. Landry had been half asleep on the bed while Tad had been watching a black-and-white monster movie on the TV with the sound turned down and subtitles on. Landry shot off the bed the moment the door clicked open. He threw himself at Gage before he'd set foot inside the room, smothering him with kisses.

"Are you okay? Any holes in you? What happened? Was it dangerous?"

Gage used his hand as a gag. "I'm perfectly fine, Lan." Gage lifted him further into the room, leaving space for Ellery to join them. He went straight to Tad, drawing him into a long, thorough kiss.

"I hear you've been misbehaving, love."

"You've been misinformed." Tad wrapped his arms around Ellery but drew back when he winced.

"Sorry, sweetheart. I'm a bit battered. Be gentle with me." Ellery tugged Tad's head back by his hair. "Not too gentle, though."

"For fuck's sake, it's like being an extra in a bad porn film." Gage sat in an armchair, pulling Landry onto his lap. "Tell me you got them their own room."

"I did! The honeymoon suite was free."

Ellery lowered himself gingerly into the other armchair while Tad perched on the edge of the bed. "Excellent. Thanks, Landry."

"I reserved it for two nights because I thought you might want to rest tomorrow."

Gage patted Landry's knee. "Good idea. It's easier for the police to watch a single property. We need to be careful until we know where Volkov has gone."

"Ooh, is that the bad guy?" Landry asked.

"Yes, love, he's not a nice man."

"He's also after the same thing I am," Ellery added.

"The jeweled egg." Landry snuggled against Gage's chest. "We need to find it before he does, don't we?"

"That would be nice," Ellery said. "Nicer would be if you have some hard liquor in your mini fridge. I'm badly in need of a drink."

Tad took it upon himself to investigate and returned with two miniature bottles of white wine. "No spirits. It's this or ginger ale."

"I'm sure room service could deliver something," Gage said. "And you've had pain meds, remember?"

Ellery was already chugging one of the bottles. He finished it then downed the other one. "Unless you two are offering a foursome, I'm going to take Tad to bed. Everything else can wait until tomorrow." Ellery lurched to his feet. "Liquid anesthesia, nice. You two be good now. Don't do anything I wouldn't."

"And that excludes what, exactly?" Gage grumbled. "I'll walk you to your room."

"It's one floor up, room fourteen," Landry offered.

"I don't want you getting fucking kidnapped between here and the next floor. I'm not chasing your tail around the countryside again."

"I may need you to help me take another bath," Ellery said, smirking.

"Gage, what's he talking about?" Landry squeaked as Gage lifted him onto the bed. "Gage?"

"Ellery, I will beat you. I told you not to mention that."

"I'm not good at taking orders." Ellery was halfway out the door, Tad in tow. "I think you should tell Landry all about it."

"I do too!" Landry said.

"Fuck my life." Gage followed Ellery. "Landry, get naked. I won't be long."

Landry undressed then wriggled beneath the covers. He couldn't wait to find out what Ellery had been talking about.

184

Gage wasn't gone long and when he returned, he was still grumbling under his breath. He stripped, climbed into bed next to Landry then lay there, tense and stiff as a log.

"Everything okay?" Landry asked, knowing full well it was far from it.

"That man could rile up a saint."

Landry stroked Gage's biceps. "It's okay that you're worried about him."

"He put you in danger. That's unacceptable."

"You realize he wanted you here helping just as much as me, don't you?"

"Rubbish. He wants in your pants, not mine." Gage pulled Landry closer.

"Are you sure about that? Ellery relishes a challenge. Are you going to tell me about this bath?"

"I'm gonna have nightmares about it and Ellery's never letting it go."

"Tell me!"

"When we found him, he was bordering on hypothermia. The medic decided a bath would be the quickest way to raise his core temperature, and Ellery insisted I should be the one to supervise."

"Was he...?"

"Yes, Lan, he was naked. I had to stand in the bath to stop him from drowning. I kept my clothes on."

"Wow. So is he...I mean...?"

"He was very cold."

Landry sniggered. "Sorry, that's not funny."

"You're telling me. I should have let him turn into a Popsicle."

"But he's okay, right?"

"He's resilient, I'll give him that. He'd taken a lot of punishment and no, I'm not giving you details because you'd have nightmares."

"Then why isn't he in a hospital?"

"Because he's a stubborn asshole, that's why."

"Because you would have checked yourself in without a fuss, wouldn't you?" Landry didn't bother to hide his skepticism.

"That's different."

"Uh-huh. You two are more alike than you realize."

"Go to sleep, Landry."

"Don't you have a punishment to give out?"

"Too tired right now. It'll keep."

Landry chuckled. "Spoon me?" Gage curled around him, warm and strong. "You're my safe place, you know?"

"Always."

Chapter Sixteen

Landry slept hard and clawed his way back to consciousness with some reluctance. Gage was missing, but when Landry patted his side of the bed it was still warm. He emerged from the bathroom a moment later, naked, hair mussed and sporting an impressive erection.

"Ooh, treat time!" Landry said, licking his lips.

"I didn't mean to wake you," Gage said, "but my mouth was so dry I needed a glass of water. That progressed to cleaning my teeth." He yawned, then stretched, showing off his abs and making his cock bounce. "You were asleep with your mouth open, and it was so tempting to stick this in there." He fisted his shaft, grinning. "I was gonna take a shower but..."

Landry scrambled out of bed, dropped to his knees in front of Gage then grabbed a couple handfuls of firm ass, pulling him closer. "C'mere." He kissed Gage's belly then sucked up a hickey. He nudged Gage's dick with his cheek. "You smell so good."

"Hands behind your back," Gage ordered, his voice gruff.

Landry clasped his hands together, lacing his fingers. He took Gage's cock into his mouth, licking under the ridge and around the tip.

"Fuck, Lan." Gage gripped his hair, holding him in place.

Landry took him deep then pulled away slowly, letting his teeth lightly graze the skin. He nuzzled Gage's balls, breathing in his scent. He licked his inner thighs, eliciting a groan.

"So good."

Landry could sense that Gage was straining to hold back his orgasm. He concentrated on the sensitive tip of Gage's dick, sucking and swirling his tongue. Gage's body convulsed as his orgasm hit. He dragged Landry close, pushing his pulsing shaft into Landry's throat. Landry swallowed, enjoying the stretch of his lips and the weight on his tongue as Gage softened.

"Jesus." Gage's legs were shaking. Landry guided him to sit down on the edge of the bed and knelt in front of him. "That was electric. Think I forgot who and where I was for a minute there."

Landry preened. "Why thank you."

"Get yourself off. I wanna watch."

Landry didn't need to be told twice. He wanted to make it last, give Gage a show. He tightened his grip as he stroked toward his body then loosened it as he moved away. He shuddered, twisting his grip as he stroked. He dug his nail into his tip and came with a cry, body shaking.

"Very nice." Gage helped him onto the bed and for a few minutes they both lay there, breathing heavily. "And hot."

"What time is it?" Landry asked. "Did we sleep late?"

"Well, I think we're gonna need brunch rather than breakfast. It's almost midday."

"Brunch sounds perfect. Will you order something while I grab a quick shower?"

"Sure. I need a minute, though." Gage had a blissed-out smile on his face.

"Can I have waffles? They do those here, right? I have a craving."

"I'm pretty sure there are waffles in England," Gage said. "I'll do my best to provide for you."

"Sarcasm is unbecoming in a Dom." Landry wiggled out of Gage's grip, energized by the stimulating start to his morning.

"Talking back is unbecoming in a sub. How do you feel about being gagged for the rest of the day?"

"I don't!" Landry ran for the shower. Hunger was riding him hard so he didn't take long. He threw on jeans and a soft sweater while Gage took his turn in the bathroom. By the time he was done, brunch had arrived and so had Tad and Ellery.

"What are you wearing?" Gage asked Ellery, grinning.

"A hotel bathrobe. What does it look like?"

"What have you got on under it?"

"Wouldn't you like to know?" Ellery smirked and began to loosen the belt.

"Stop right there, mister."

"You are so boring. This was a preferable option to the police issue sweats I came back here in last night. Those things are going in the incinerator. I have nothing else to wear. Tad only had what he was wearing yesterday and besides, his clothes are too small for me."

"Fuck's sake. There was nothing wrong with those sweats. You can borrow something of mine." Gage pushed Ellery toward the wardrobe. While he picked out an outfit, Gage ordered more food. "If you know what's good for you, you'll change in the bathroom."

Laughing, Ellery changed behind a closed door then emerged in jeans that were a decent fit and a cream sweater that was a bit tight on Gage but fitted him perfectly.

"You look like shit," Gage commented to Ellery. "And I'm not talking about my clothes."

The second food order arrived, and they all settled around the table.

"Thanks." Ellery downed a glass of orange juice. "I feel like it but couldn't stay in bed any longer. We need to take advantage of Volkov being at something of a disadvantage for once and plan our next steps. My brain isn't functioning at one hundred percent, so we came down here to prod the hive mind."

"You're not prodding anything of mine, Ellery." Gage stabbed the air with his fork, a strip of bacon waving precariously.

Ellery smirked. "One day, Gage. You don't know what you're missing."

"Should have left you in that fucking storeroom. Out of sight and out of my fucking mind."

"You're quiet, Tad," Landry said. "You okay?"

"I don't want anyone else to get hurt. Apart from Volkov — him I want to hurt."

Ellery reached for Tad's hand and gave it a squeeze. "My sweet, violent boy."

"What *does* happen next?" Landry asked. "Aren't your cop buddies on the case now?"

"They'll be hunting Volkov for kidnapping and they'll want to talk to him about the Ascott family deaths," Gage said, "but they won't be looking for the egg. They don't have the manpower to go treasure hunting for something that might not exist."

"So we should carry on looking," Landry said, excited. "Though I'm not sure how." He dug through his pile of waffles. "These are so good!" No one responded and he looked up to find three men staring at him.

"What?"

"Have you not eaten this week?" Tad asked.

"I thought I was the one being held captive on starvation rations," Ellery commented.

Gage just grinned and munched another piece of bacon.

"I've had an energy expending morning, okay?" Landry pouted before shoving another strawberry-laden piece of waffle in his mouth.

"I'll just bet you have." Ellery stared at Gage.

"A gentleman never tells, but he did earn his waffles."

Landry's cell rang, and he leaned across to the bedside cabinet to reach it, almost toppling off his chair in the process. Gage righted him with a sigh.

"Oh, it's Petey! It must be late there." He answered the call, listened for a while then yelled at his friend. "Slow down, Petey. I'm gonna put you on the speaker. Start again and talk slow, okay?"

"Okay." Petey's voice filled the room. "Hi, everyone."

There was a chorus of greetings before Gage asked, "Is Carson with you?"

"He's here. So are Sorrell and Tank. We've been working on your mystery."

"You roped in half of Seattle?" Ellery asked.

"Sure did. We're like the Scooby gang." Landry beamed.

"I don't know what to say." Ellery made exasperated gestures at Gage who shrugged and carried on eating.

"Tell everyone what you told me, Petey," Landry instructed.

"Well, it's Saturday, Sunday now actually. After work we were going to go out but the weather here is a poopfest so we had a picnic in the apartment instead."

"Petey...get to the point!" Landry yelled.

"Sorry. Scene setting. We were all full of food and lazy. I showed everyone the picture you sent of the stained-glass window, and we all took turns in coming up with ideas. Most of them were garbage, have to say, but...drum roll please..."

"Petey!" Landry's voice was accompanied by Tad's, Ellery's and Gage's.

"You're all so impatient. I got to thinking about the hens. Why three, not one? There's only supposed to be one inside the egg, isn't there?"

"Yes, just the one," Ellery confirmed.

"They were an addition to the original window design so there had to be a reason for them."

Ellery started to look interested, sitting forward in his chair.

"You told me that the original name of the Ascott family was Aucourte," Petey continued, "which is French. It didn't take much research to discover that the three French hens, from the Twelve Days of Christmas, stand for faith, love and hope. That matches up with the relationship in the letter Ellery found."

"You might be on to something," Ellery said.

"That's not all. Landry said the family also had a townhouse in Chelsea and that Edgar was still living there until he passed away. We all thought that it would have been far too obvious for Frederick Ascott to hide the egg in a property he owned but only one street away there's a pub called Les Trois Poules, I found it on a street map."

"The Three Hens. Bloody hell." Ellery's eyes gleamed.

"Wait, wait, wait. There's more. Oh my God, I'm too excited. You tell them, Carson."

"Hi, all." Carson's deep tones sounded over the speaker. "We went down a few blind alleys to get here but we found out that the Russian Revolution of 1917 led to a large wave of Russian immigration to England. Most of them were running from the violence and instability of the new Soviet regime. They came from a variety of backgrounds. Some were wealthy aristocrats who had lost their fortunes while others were working-class people seeking a better life. The immigrants settled all over England, but the largest concentrations were in London.

"A man called Konstantin Gusev arrived in London with his French wife. He bought a property in Chelsea, opened an inn and called it Les Trois Poules. I'd guess faith, hope and love meant something to him, too. We figure it's not much of a stretch to think that Frederick Ascott might have formed a connection with him, considering their shared backgrounds."

"And that could be where he hid the egg!" Landry was so excited he knocked over the phone. "Oops, sorry, I dropped you all." He righted it.

"You think we could have something?" Sorrell's voice piped up.

"I think you guys are incredible," Ellery said. "It's definitely worth looking into."

"Can we go to bed now?" That was Tank. "It's nearly four."

"I won't be able to sleep," Sorrell said.

"Not a problem. There are plenty of things I can do with you while you're horizontal."

"Uh, you guys are still on speaker," Landry pointed out, then the call disconnected.

He was going to call back, but Gage stopped him. "Leave them be. It's real late there. We can get back to them when we have any news."

"We have to go to this place, right, Gage?" Landry said. "We can't stop now."

"I'm not sure it's a good idea, love. I don't want you getting your hopes up, this could all be a wild goose chase."

"It could," Ellery agreed, "but isn't it fun finding out?"

"I don't call being held prisoner and tortured fun." Gage glared at Ellery.

"Wait, what?" Landry gaped. "Nobody mentioned anything about torture. What the hell?"

"Well, fuck. It wasn't something you needed to know, sweetheart. Me and my big mouth."

"I suppose you all know except me." Landry stamped his foot. "I am not some delicate flower. I found a dead body in my store doorway and didn't have a meltdown. Okay, I had a small meltdown, nothing major, but that's not the point. If Tad knows stuff then I get to know, too."

"It was no big deal, Landry," Ellery said. "I'm fine."

"No, you're not!" Tad shouted then he scowled. "He was beaten up, whipped and half frozen. He has bruised ribs, and you can see what they did to his face, his back is wrecked, and he has a cut on his arm."

"To be fair, I did that last one myself," Ellery admitted. "Caught it on a nail when I was sneaking around Volkov's yard."

"It's infected. You're only functioning because you're dosed up on painkillers and antibiotics."

"They might have killed you," Landry whispered, his lip wobbling. He was picking up on Tad's obvious distress.

"Gage, don't let him cry. Seriously. Hug him or something." Ellery's expression was panicked.

Gage patted Landry's hand. "Honey, it'd take a lot more than that to kill him. He's tougher than my old work boots. Believe me, I've thought about it often enough."

Landry sniffled. "Okay, but while the jeweled egg is still out there, we're all in danger. Finding it is the only way this is all gonna stop."

"You're not going to let this go, are you?" Gage pulled Landry onto his lap.

"Not in a million years."

Gage ruffled his hair. "Then I guess you and I are taking a trip to Chelsea."

"Yay! We're going on an adventure."

"One that I fear will have to involve just the two of you this time," Ellery said, "I'm not really up to going anywhere today, much as it pains me to admit it."

"I wouldn't allow it anyway," Gage said. "You've got a massive target painted on your back already. You're confined to quarters with orders to rest. Maybe you can get Tad to feed you grapes or something."

"I think I'll be feeding him, actually, but not with grapes."

Tad rolled his eyes, but his lip quirked as if he were trying not to smile. "I'll make sure he stays here, don't worry."

"Tad, do I remember you saying that you and Ellery share a flat in Chelsea?"

"We do."

"We could run by there and pick up some clothes for you both, couldn't we, Gage?"

"I guess so. If it's not too much of a detour. In fact, it would be good to see if anyone is watching your place, Ellery."

"Landry needs to be the one to pick out my outfits, not you." Ellery brushed a non-existent piece of lint from the sweater he had borrowed.

"I have good taste in clothes," Gage protested.

"If you're picking things out for chasing criminals down the back alleys of Seattle maybe."

"Landry, help me out here." Gage jiggled Landry in his lap.

"He's kinda right. I mean, I love you and I love everything you wear, but you do tend to go for practicality. You have plaid shirts in your wardrobe, Gage."

Tad snorted with laughter. "You looked great in leather the other night, you should wear more of that, Gage."

"Yeah, I can hear the comments now if I showed up to the precinct in leather pants. Fine, Landry picks out the clothes. What are the opening hours for this three chickens place? It's all a bit random here on a Sunday."

"Hens, not chickens."

"Same difference, Lan. It's all poultry."

"The plot chickens?" Landry giggled.

"No fowl language?" Tad contributed.

"We're going to need the best of cluck!"

"Christ, stop them, Roskam! This is more excruciating than getting whipped." Ellery shifted in his seat, clearly uncomfortable and in no small amount of pain.

"Sorry," Landry said. "I couldn't help myself."

Tad grinned at him then scowled at Ellery. "I'm taking your stubborn ass back to bed. You should never have gotten up in the first place. Let Landry and Gage do their thing for a few hours. It won't kill you to rest, even though I know it's against your religion."

"You're all ganging up on me," Ellery complained, but it was half-hearted.

"You're white as milk, Ellery. Go to bed," Gage snapped.

"And there's a phrase I never thought I'd hear coming out of your mouth."

"Leave my mouth out of this conversation," Gage growled. "Tad, take him away before I damage him further." Tad obliged and Gage turned to Landry. "Do I need to tell you to behave today? You do what I say, when I say it."

"Yes, Sir! Absolutely. I'll be so good."

"Hmm. Still tempted to put you on a lead."

"We can so do that when we get back!"

Gage shook his head, but Landry could tell he had him hooked. It was going to be an interesting day.

Chapter Seventeen

Les Trois Poules turned out to be one of those buildings that looked a little out of place. It was clearly older than its Georgian neighbors, with bowed walls and leaded windows with small diamond panes. Landry and Gage had taken a black cab from Soho, and Landry now stood on the sidewalk admiring the building's façade while Gage paid the fare.

"This place is so cute. Look at the sign." Landry pointed at the board jutting out from the building on a cast-iron frame. "The way the three hens are pecking at the ground is remarkably similar to the ones in the stained-glass window."

"Too similar to be coincidental," Gage agreed.

"The building looks real old. The Russian dude must have moved into a pre-existing place."

"Most of this city is older than dirt," Gage said. "The Brits think anything under two hundred years old is modern."

"Petey told me that London is one of the oldest cities in the world. It dates back two thousand years or more. The Romans were here first. He told me lots of other stuff and dates, but I can't remember any of it now. I wish I'd listened to him better."

"How about we go take a look inside instead of standing on the sidewalk," Gage suggested.

"Good plan. Look, there's a little rainbow sticker in the window, that's a good sign." Landry grabbed Gage's hand and dragged him inside.

Stepping through the door was like being transported back in time. Landry breathed in the scents of brass polish and beer. Dark varnished wooden panels lined the walls, and the floor was stone. There was a bar to one side and a restaurant area to the other. Gage opted for the bar. The space was dominated by an imposing counter made of some kind of dark wood. Behind the bar, a barman with an impressive beard and mustache was pulling pints for patrons standing two deep. Shelves above the bar were laden with an assortment of bottles, the contents a riot of colors.

The seating was arranged in a variety of nooks and crannies. There were small round tables, high-backed wooden chairs and benches, plus a few armchairs and several stools by an open fireplace. The walls were decorated with an eclectic mix of memorabilia, a lot of it brass and copper, interspersed with framed black-and-white photographs.

Landry spotted a couple finishing their drinks and did a rapid shimmy toward their now vacant table.

"Impressive moves, love. I thought we'd be standing at the bar."

"The benefits of fighting for space in various Seattle coffee houses," Landry said. "You snooze you lose."

"What would you like to drink?"

"Orange soda, please. I need something sweet and fizzy."

"Like you ever need an injection of sugar." Shaking his head, Gage made his way to the bar and inserted himself between two groups of people. His height gave him an advantage, and he was served quickly. He was soon back to the table with their drinks.

"What did you get?" Landry asked, dipping a finger into Gage's glass, which contained an amber colored liquid.

"It's a guest beer they had on tap. Some kind of real ale. As I'm off duty, I thought I'd try it." He took a long drink then wiped foam from his lips with the back of his hand. "Nice. Could be colder."

Landry licked his finger. "Oh, icky." He sipped his soda through a stripy paper straw. "Much better. I wonder how many times this place has been remodeled in the last hundred years."

"Several times, I'd guess. It would have to have been brought up to code as regulations changed over the years."

"So what are the chances that something hidden here wouldn't have been found?"

Gage sipped his beer. "I don't know love, but I think this Ascott guy would have been very careful in choosing a spot. You have to admit the clues he left were obscure and it was pure chance that Ellery found that letter and worked out the potential implication of it."

"I wonder why he hid the egg at all."

"From what Ellery says, it's an exceptionally rare thing, worth a huge amount of money. Even a hundred years ago it would have been valuable. Once Ascott knew that his lover wouldn't be joining him, who knows what was going through his head. Back then there may have been others hunting the egg. If it had such sentimental value for him, he wouldn't have wanted it found but maybe he didn't want to look at it either. It would have been a painful reminder of what he'd lost, after all. He tucked it away for a future generation to track down and left them clues to help."

"The whole story is so tragic. I can't imagine what emotional turmoil he must have been going through at the time knowing that he'd left Yelizabeta behind in Russia. That he'd survived while she was killed."

"It was a long time ago, Landry, don't get upset."

"I guess I'm a bit emotional, too, after everything that happened to Ellery. I dread to think what Volkov would have done to him if you hadn't found him."

"What-ifs don't help anything, love. We found him, that's what counts."

"How do you think this Volkov dude got to know what Ellery was up to?"

"No idea, but maybe Ellery can enlighten us. There are some worrying aspects to all this. Ellery overheard something that indicates a leak inside the Metropolitan police. That's how Volkov and his men got away when we went to find Ellery. If Volkov's reach is that long, who knows how many other spies he has?

"Also, from what you've told me, the missing Fabergé eggs are one of those hidden treasure urban legends. He could have already been hunting them down and crossed paths with Ellery by accident. Ellery would have had to have asked questions to get as far as he did on the trail. He wouldn't have been able to keep all his activities secret. He also has a reputation, so Volkov would probably have already had him on his radar."

"He did recover that note in the first place when he was searching for a Russian bracelet, didn't he?"

"This plot is like a spider web, intricate but sticky. Not something you want to walk into in the dark."

Landry shuddered. "I hate when that happens. I swear spiders build webs in our yard deliberately so that I walk through them."

"They set webs to catch prey, Lan. And you probably look very, very tasty." Gage grinned.

Landry stuck his tongue out at him. "You're the detective, how would you go about finding out more about this place?"

"Well, I'd start off by asking the people who work here but I think we have to be a bit more subtle than that."

"Oh, leave that to me."

Landry touched the arm of a passing server who was balancing a tray of empty glasses. "Hey, can you spare a moment?"

"Sure, what can I do for you?"

"Well, we're over here from the States. We were taking a walk from our hotel when we came across this place. It's so quaint. Do you have any information on its history?"

"Sure, we get asked a lot. Give me a minute, and I'll fetch you a pamphlet."

"Bless your heart."

The server made his way between the tables to the bar.

"Laying it on a bit thick, aren't you?" Gage said. "What's with the southern accent?"

"I have no idea what you mean," Landry said. "Nobody here is going to remember a couple American tourists asking questions, are they?"

"You're not just a pretty face, are you?"

The server dropped off the pamphlet on his way to deliver drinks to another table. Landry grabbed it. He scanned it through then sighed. "I think we're onto a dead end here."

"How so?"

"Take a look at the last page." Landry pushed the pamphlet toward Gage. "It says that the entire property was gutted by fire in 1924. It was restored using original methods and materials but had to be taken back to bare brick. If there had been anything hidden here, it would have been found then."

"Damn." Gage flicked through the pamphlet. "I really thought we might be onto something. The Russian immigrant that bought the place after the revolution even gets a mention."

Landry tried to hide his disappointment, but he couldn't help but feel downcast. "What about a cellar, that wouldn't have been damaged by fire." The server, who was making another circuit of the room, stopped by the table.

"Sorry, I couldn't help but overhear. We don't have a cellar here. None of the properties in this street do because they're too close to the river and would have been permanently flooded. We store the beer in a cold room out back. It's solid stone and maintains a constant temperature."

"When was that put in?" Gage asked.

"Late 1920s, if I recall correctly. Then it was used as a bomb shelter in the Second World War. Earth was piled on top of it so it's kind of buried in the backyard." At a shout from the barman, he scurried off.

Gage swallowed what was left of his beer. "I hate to say it but we're getting nowhere fast here. How about we go check out Ellery's place?"

"Okay. I have to admit I'm really curious. I wonder what his interior decoration style is."

"Florals," Gage said, chuckling. "Lots of florals."

"You're terrible!"

"So what are you thinking?" Gage put their empty glasses back on the bar then they made their way outside. Landry blinked in the bright light.

"I'm picturing a boudoir. Lots of dark red and gold. Extravagant. Nothing but the best."

Gage pulled up a map on his cell. "His building is about ten minutes' walk from here."

"This is a real upscale area," Landry said, peering at the display in a realtor's window. "We're talking price tags in the millions of pounds."

Gage leaned over his shoulder. "I thought the prices in Seattle were highway robbery. We couldn't afford a bedsit around here."

"Do you think Ellery's family have money, or does he really do that well for himself hunting down stolen objects?"

"Could be both, but who's to say what Ellery finds when he locates stuff. He's employed to find certain things insured by his company, but I can't imagine stuff like that is stolen in isolation."

"What are you saying? You think Ellery is a thief?" Landry looped his arm through Gage's.

"I wouldn't put anything past him."

Ellery had given Gage the access code to his building, which Gage punched in. Ellery's apartment was on the top floor and there was no elevator, so Landry and Gage walked up. The stairs and corridors were all carpeted, the walls painted in a calming shade of sage green.

"This place is plush," Landry commented.

"Did you expect anything else?" Gage responded. He had two more codes to enter and only then did he take out Ellery's key. He opened the door, the lone one on their floor. "This is the penthouse."

"Of course it is." Landry took a step inside, mouth open. "Is this floor marble?"

"I believe it is," Gage said, "probably imported from Italy. I can't believe he has a fucking chandelier in his hallway."

Landry found a light switch then turned it on so that he could admire the glittering cascade of crystals. "Wow. That's an antique that's been converted to electricity, it's absolutely gorgeous." He poked his head around the door to what proved to be a living room. Floor-to-ceiling windows with deep red velvet drapes framed a view of the skyline. There were two luxurious sofas arranged in front of an impressive fireplace and despite the somewhat ostentatious display of wealth, it felt cozy. Books were piled haphazardly on a low table, a pot plant sat on a windowsill and a pair of boots stuck out from the side of a chair. Each wall displayed impressive landscape paintings, and Landry peered at the signature on one. "Holy fuck, this is a Turner!"

"What's one of those worth?" Gage asked. "It's a bit gloomy."

"The auction record for a Turner is around forty-five million dollars and that was a while back."

"Why the heck does Ellery work at all?"

"The thrill of it, I suppose. You'd be the same if you won the lottery."

"Well, we'd know if somebody had been in here to turn the place over," Gage said. "There's no sign of forced entry or damage anywhere so far. Let's find the bedroom so we can pack some clothes."

Landry closed the door to the living room then ventured along the corridor. He came to the kitchen next, then a bathroom. That left two doors. "This feels like one of those riddles — which door to pick," he said. Gage took the initiative and went to the one on the left.

"Oh my God, this was not the right choice."

Landry nudged him aside to take a look. "Wow! They have a dungeon in their spare bedroom." The decor was much more utilitarian than in the lounge, with blackout curtains, matte black walls and a dark laminate floor. The main feature of the room was a black steel four poster draped with translucent curtains.

"That must have been made to order," Gage muttered.

"I love it!" Landry ran his hands across the black sheet. "This feels like silk."

"Everything in here is high-end. That spanking bench is one of the best I've ever seen and I'd love to get you in one of those punishment chairs."

"There are so many permutations for positions," Landry said. "This place is making me hard."

"Time to move on," Gage said. "I'm not giving Ellery any fantasy material."

The second bedroom was luxurious but normal — if normal included handcuffs dangling from the headboard and the spreader bar poking out from beneath the bed. "I'm afraid to look in the closet," Landry said. "But I guess we have to. Tad said there'd be an overnight bag in the bottom."

Gage found the bag then Landry spent some time picking out clothes from the closet and a large dresser until he had enough for three days or so for both Ellery and Tad. "You think I should pack Tad's rubber underwear?" Landry dangled the skimpy garment from one finger.

"Definitely." Gage chuckled. "Ellery is in no condition to get up to much so that will annoy him, which will make my day."

"So bad." Landry threw in a few more pairs of kinky underwear. "I think we're done. Shall we head back?"

"Yeah. We need to plan what we're going to do next and we can't do that here. Also, we still have to discuss your punishment for riding off into the wilds of England with Tad."

"I thought you'd forgotten about that," Landry muttered. He handed Gage the overnight bag.

"When have I ever forgotten a punishment?"

"Never." Landry sighed. "What's it going to be?"

"We'll discuss it on the walk back. I was contemplating banning you from drinking coffee for a few days, what do you think about that?"

"I don't think you'd be that cruel. You wouldn't, would you? Gage?"

"Make sure you lock the door properly."

Landry turned the key then twisted the door handle just to make sure. He handed the keys back to Gage, who pocketed them. "Gage? Don't keep me hanging. The whole coffee thing would be far too cruel. Punishment should be proportionate to the crime, you always say. Gage!"

Gage was humming happily to himself as they descended the stairs. "It's the small things that give a Dom joy."

Chapter Eighteen

"So what did you think of our home sweet home?" Ellery smirked.

"Next time, tell a person which door to go through. We could all have avoided a good deal of trauma." Gage handed the bag of clothes to Tad. "I may never recover. I'm sending you my therapy bills. And what's with all the damn codes?"

"To turn off the laser grid, the pressure plates, the cameras and the killer bees."

"Figures."

"You loved it, didn't you?"

"It was…something."

"I loved it," Landry whispered to Tad.

"Of course you did." Tad rifled through the bag then shared a conspiratorial grin with Landry. "Bad boy."

"Not as bad as you!"

"I do enjoy the cling of rubber in the morning."

"Latex was a top ten invention, that's for sure."

"When you two have stopped whispering," Gage said, "we have things to discuss and I'm not talking about the furnishings in your spare room, Ellery."

"How does dinner in the hotel restaurant sound?" Ellery suggested. "Say in an hour?"

"Deal." Gage took Landry's hand. "We have unfinished business. An hour should be plenty of time."

"For what, Gage?" Landry let Gage tug him toward the elevator. "You're so mean to me!"

By the time they reached their room, Landry was desperate to know how Gage intended to punish him.

How bad can it be? He's a big squishy marshmallow under that scowly exterior, and I wasn't that bad.

Once inside their room, Gage put out the 'Do not disturb' sign then locked the door. "Strip, then get on your knees, mister." Landry's clothes went flying in all directions. He knelt at Gage's feet, head bowed. "Tell me why you're being punished."

"I disobeyed you, Sir. I put myself in danger by doing something I knew you wouldn't approve of. I didn't tell you what I was doing when I know I should have."

"That's right. You need to understand, Landry, that I love you more than life. Not being around to protect you is not acceptable to me when there's an alternative. This punishment is for disobedience and for scaring your Dom. Your safe word still applies."

"Yes, Sir." Gage sounded so serious. Landry was already on the verge of tears. He hated disappointing Gage.

"Ellery recommended I pick one of these up and I'm glad I did." Gage took something from a drawer. "Stand up." Landry managed a graceful move from kneeling to standing. "It's a cock ring and butt plug all in one."

"No need to sound quite so pleased about it," Landry muttered as Gage passed the cock ring over his cock and balls. It nestled snugly, providing pressure but not so tight it hurt. "This bit goes between your legs then with a nice coating of lube…" Gage squeezed gel over the toy. "It should go in nice and easy."

"It's big!" Landry squeaked as his hole stretched to accommodate the intruder.

"And you can take it just fine."

"Says the stuffer, not the stuffee!"

"Quiet, brat. I know your limits, and this isn't close."

"Sorry, Sir." *It does feel good.*

"Okay. Sit at the table."

Landry groaned at the additional pressure on his butt. Gage put the newspaper that was left outside their door each day, on the table along with a pen. "I want you to color in every O on this page."

"Huh?" Landry examined the dense text. *So boring!* "I'd much prefer a spanking."

"I know you would and that's why you're not getting one. This is punishment, not pleasure."

"Dang."

"Two rules. You're to do this in silence and you're not allowed to come."

"Not likely, Sir." Landry started coloring. Gage sat at the table opposite him and placed a small device on the table. He pressed a button and the plug inside Landry vibrated and kept on vibrating.

Landry sucked his breath. His hand shook as he attempted to color in letters and his dick grew rigid. Gage checked his watch. "Fifteen minutes. Remember, no talking and no coming." He laid his cell on the table and from what Landry could see, started playing Candy Crush.

He's evil. I had no idea he could be this evil. I'm gonna die.

His face heated along with his groin. He wriggled, trying to shift the pressure inside his ass to a less stimulating position but only managed to make it worse. The cock ring seemed to be getting tighter. Gage had managed to construct the perfect punishment. A boring task, a gag order and agonizing sexual frustration. Even worse, Gage wasn't taking any apparent notice of Landry's predicament.

After fifteen minutes, Landry was sobbing, desperate to come and prepared to swear to the coffee gods that he would never be bad again.

Gage turned off the vibrator. "Punishment over."

"Bits of me are gonna explode!" Landry wailed. "Sir, help me!" He dropped his pen, which rolled off the table. He'd only filled a third of the letter Os on the page. The cock ring was the only thing stopping him from coming like Old Faithful.

Gage scooped him off his chair then tossed him onto the bed. With a few deft movements he removed the plug and cock ring. Landry made a grab for his cock, jerked it twice then came with a scream. After a few panting breaths, he lay in a boneless heap. "That's better!"

"Did I say you could come?" Gage flicked the tip of Landry's ultra-sensitive cock.

"It just happened, Sir! I couldn't help it."

"Zero self-control."

"Next time, could you just spank me? I'll promise not to enjoy it."

"Next time?" Gage rolled Landry onto his front and delivered a few hard smacks to his ass.

"Ow! Slip of the tongue," Landry protested. "Cos there won't be a next time. Ever!"

"To be honest, I thought you'd use your safe word after five minutes. I'm quite impressed you took the whole punishment." Gage sat on the bed next to him.

"It was horrible." Landry crawled onto Gage's lap and snuggled against his chest. "It's scary how well you know me."

"Remember that if you get any more escapades into that pretty head of yours." Gage petted him, held him and muttered soothing words of forgiveness into his ear. "I love you."

"I love you, too." Landry felt dozy and content. Gage was so good at after-care, whether following a scene or a punishment. He never rushed it or made Landry feel too needy.

After a while, Gage gave Landry's hair a little tug. "You good?"

Landry gave an affirmative murmur. "Sticky but good."

"We should get ready for dinner with Ellery and Tad. Why don't you go grab a shower?"

"Okay." Landry ambled into the bathroom then went through the motions of getting clean. He put on a clean pair of jeans and a dark shirt. Gage had already changed, and Landry wanted to crawl beneath Gage's sweater so that they could be skin to skin.

"Stop looking at me like I'm edible," Gage scolded.

"You look good enough to eat right now." Landry pulled on red and white striped socks and his black smarter shoes.

"The socks are an interesting touch," Gage said.

"Aren't they cool? I have a pair in yellow and black, too. I'm good to go. I could eat an entire lasagna, or a roast chicken." He ran his tongue across his lower lip whilst staring at Gage's groin. "Or something equally tasty."

"Jesus, Landry, stop that! I don't want to be sitting through dinner with James fucking Ellery sporting a hard-on."

"Too late." Landry grinned then dropped to his knees in front of Gage. It was a matter of seconds to lower Gage's zipper and release his straining cock. Landry didn't bother with teasing, he took Gage deep and sucked hard.

"Fuck!" Gage grabbed Landry's hair. "Your mouth is a lethal weapon." He pushed into Landry's throat and Landry swallowed. With a few uncontrolled jerks of his hips, Gage came in a hot gush. Landry took it all before planting a few soft kisses across Gage's exposed belly.

"Yum!"

Gage tugged him to his feet. He tucked his cock away then zipped up. "I'm convinced you're the devil disguised as an angel."

"I'm gonna take that as a compliment." Landry ran a hand through his mussed hair, giving it a cursory tidy. "Shall we go, because that only counts as an appetizer, and I'm even hungrier now?"

Downstairs, the restaurant was buzzing. Tad and Ellery were already seated at a corner table and there was a bottle of wine in an ice bucket to Ellery's side. Tad was perusing the menu and sipping from a glass of water. Gage took the seat next to Ellery, so Tad was next to Landry.

"Good evening, gentlemen. The two of you look… content." Ellery tilted his head to one side. "I think you made good use of the hour since we were last together."

Landry's face heated as his head filled with images of what he and Gage had been up to. Ellery's expression said he had a good idea what that might have been.

"Give me the fucking menu, Ellery," Gage said.

Landry leaned across so that he could share with Tad.

"Did he punish you hard?" Tad whispered.

"It wasn't fun, but once it was done, things got way better," Landry whispered back. "You?"

"Ellery is evil in the best way."

Landry snorted with laughter but gulped as he saw the number of menu choices on offer. He gave Gage a panicked glance.

"You want me to pick for you, sweetheart?"

Landry nodded, relieved. Too many yummy choices meant decisions under pressure, something he wasn't good at.

Ellery and Gage placed their orders with the waiter then Ellery poured Gage a glass of wine. Landry opted for water.

"So I take it that your trip to Les Trois Poules was unsuccessful," Ellery said, his French accent impeccable.

"It was a great place, but there's no chance that anything that may once have been hidden there wouldn't already have been found," Landry said. He explained what they'd learned. "It's so disappointing. I really thought Petey and Sorrell had found us a solid lead."

"Well, while you two were off on your little day trip," Ellery said, "Tad and I weren't wasting our time."

"It's impressive what he can do with a pair of handcuffs and a blindfold," Tad whispered in Landry's ear. Landry spluttered into his water glass and had to wipe his face with a napkin.

"Remind me to never leave you two alone together, ever," Gage said.

"Agreed." Ellery clinked his glass against Gage's. "Far too much trouble for mischief."

"It's a Dom conspiracy," Tad muttered.

"If we could get back to the point, love," Ellery said. "We don't think that Les Trois Poules is a dead end just yet." He stayed quiet while their entrées were delivered then lowered his voice to continue.

"I had Tad do a bit of digging and by that, I mean hacking. You probably already know that London is riddled with tunnels and hidden passageways."

"I read about ghost underground stations when I was planning our trip," Landry said. "That was really interesting."

"That's right, Landry. There are actually a lot of different kinds of tunnels beneath the city serving various purposes. Some of them are transport routes for pedestrians. There are government bunkers used during the war and there's even a tunnel under the river. It got me thinking that we should take a look at what might be hidden under our feet in Chelsea."

Landry fidgeted, excited. "You found something, didn't you?"

"Maybe. It had to be something that was already out of use around the start of the last century, so it got me thinking about sewers."

"A place your mind is all too familiar with," Gage muttered. "Do carry on."

Ellery rolled his eyes. "You'd know. Anyway, as I was saying, getting hold of historic maps of the sewer system took a bit of doing."

"Their security system was dire," Tad commented. "It wasn't that hard."

"Is anyone going to get to the point any time soon?" Gage asked. "I'm not getting any younger."

"Patience," Ellery said. "Not one of your virtues, I know. What we found when we got a chance to examine the maps was a Victorian sewer outlet into the Thames directly behind the building housing Les Trois Poules. It was replaced by a much bigger pipe further along the river in about 1902, so would have been abandoned for several years by the time Frederick Ascott was looking for a hidey hole."

Their entrées were cleared and replaced by the main course. Landry took a mouthful of the prawn and asparagus risotto Gage had chosen for him. "So yum, nice choice. So we need to get a look in the tunnel, don't we?"

"Yes, we do," Ellery agreed. "It has to be worth exploring. I don't believe those other clues were set just to lead us to a dead end."

"Is it accessible?" Gage asked, ever practical.

"No idea. We had a good look for photographs of the riverbank in that area but there wasn't anything that helped. There's a path along the river but it's quite high up. There's a drop to the water. What we did find is that there's a very narrow access point to the shoreline. It was mentioned on one of those hidden London sites because it takes you down to a small beach with a great view. Of course, all the photographs that people have taken from there are of the river, not the bank."

"I don't recall seeing a path between the buildings on that street," Landry said, "but we were focused on getting to the pub. We could easily have walked right past it."

"Part of its charm is that it's well hidden. I'm not surprised you missed it. We need to go tonight," Ellery said.

"Why?" Gage asked. "Can't it wait until tomorrow? It's pitch-dark out there."

"No, I don't think it can. If there's any chance that you were followed by one of Volkov's men today, he will have had his people digging in the same places as us. He's not stupid."

"I didn't notice anyone following us," Gage said, "but if they were good enough, I was pretty distracted. It's possible, I suppose."

Landry pushed his plate away. "We're gonna need a flashlight, does anyone have one?" He got shakes of the head from around the table.

"Who said you'd be going?" Gage scowled.

"Sir! I can't miss this. We should all go."

"Ellery's still recovering."

"I'm not staying here either!" Ellery announced.

"That's settled then," Landry said. "How about I go ask Winston if the hotel has a flashlight we can borrow?"

"Okay, that's a good idea," Gage said, grudgingly. "I'll fetch a coat from the room for you. Are you sure you're up to coming with us, Ellery?"

"I wouldn't miss it. This could be our last chance to find the egg. Let's reconvene in the lobby in say, fifteen minutes? I need to change into something a bit more practical for this kind of activity."

Landry gave Gage a kiss on the cheek. "I'll see you out front."

They all dispersed, and Landry made his way to the lobby where there was a short queue at reception and a large group of people hovering, glasses in hand. Landry guessed they had spilled over from the bar where there was a private function going on. He went to see if Winston was outside in his usual spot. It was a cold evening, the sky clear with a scattering of stars visible even with London's light pollution. Landry spotted Winston on the corner of the street where it looked like he'd been giving directions to the driver of a limousine. He straightened from where he'd been leaning into the window and spotted Landry. He waved and began running in Landry's direction.

Why's he running? Landry couldn't understand why Winston was charging along the street, his long uniform coat flapping. Then something sharp pricked Landry's side, penetrating his clothing.

"If you want to survive the night, you'll come with me." The voice in Landry's ear was low and menacing. He froze but was prodded into action as the same limousine that Winston had been dealing with pulled up next to them. *It must have circled the block.* Winston was still twenty meters away.

The man with the knife shoved Landry toward the car then bundled him inside. Landry fell face down onto the seat, sprawling part way into the foot well. His legs were kicked out of the way as the other man got in beside him then the door slammed, and the car pulled away just as Winston banged on the window.

Well, dang it, this can't be good. Landry pulled himself onto the back seat and turned to face his attacker. The hat and the scarred lip were all too familiar. *Gage is gonna be so mad with me.*

Chapter Nineteen

I've had better times in handcuffs. Landry pressed himself against the car door, trying to get as far away as possible from his assailant, which wasn't far. Now he was close to him, Landry could see that Fedora Man wasn't as old as he had first thought. He wasn't great at guessing ages, but he estimated mid-to-late thirties. Reddish hair curled from beneath his hat and the puckered scar at the corner of his lip was about an inch long.

"Did you get that scar from a whip?" Landry couldn't resist asking. "Only a friend of mine had a run in with one of Mr. Volkov's lion-taming associates recently. I suppose he had to practice somewhere."

"If you know anything about Mr. Volkov, you should also know you'd be better off keeping your mouth shut."

To Landry's surprise, the man's accent was Scottish, not Russian. "So he flew off on his private jet and left you behind to do his dirty work, did he? Charming."

Fedora Man scowled. "Fortunately, he's made following you around worth my while. You've been a fucking pain in the ass. I nearly had you at the museum. Then that interfering doorman at your hotel started fucking with me. I suppose that was your doing?"

"No idea what you're talking about."

"Fifty quid a time for information on your whereabouts and it took me three days to realize he was yanking my chain. He sent me all the way to fucking Kew Gardens to look at trees, had me craning my neck on the London Eye, then the final nail in what will hopefully be your coffin, was searching Highgate Cemetery." He snarled. "And I could have done without tracking you around the gay sex shops of Soho."

Winston, you star! "Was Highgate interesting? I definitely want to take a tour there."

"I'm gonna enjoy skewering you. In the end, you did most of the work for us. The pub was an obscure link."

"If it makes you feel better, you did a good job tracking us there. My boyfriend didn't spot you and he's a detective."

"You should check the license number of the black cab drivers that pick you up. I didn't need to follow you because I knew where you were going. Mr. Volkov had people working on why Les Trois Poules might be important and here we are. You didn't find the egg in the building so someone put the clues together."

Landry sighed. "You realize I still don't know exactly where the egg is. This could be another dead end."

"The tunnels under London have been used by criminal gangs for years. You're going to find this one for me. Then we'll see."

"And if I don't?"

"I'll start making inconvenient holes in your body."

"That doesn't sound like something I'd enjoy. What if I find the tunnel but the egg isn't there?"

"Then you and I will be taking a little plane ride to visit Mr. Volkov and the idiot that did this to me" — he touched his lip—"can get more practice on *you*."

Oh...please hurry, Gage.

The limo pulled up just past Les Trois Poules. "Put this over your hands." Fedora Man shoved a woolen scarf at Landry. "You scream or yell, and I'll make sure you don't do it again." He got out of the car, walked around it then opened the door on Landry's side. "Out."

Landry twisted the scarf around his wrists like a muffler, covering the cuffs. Fedora Man stood behind him while the driver stayed in the limo. "I'm not unaware that your friends won't be far behind us so no delaying tactics, understand?"

Landry was pretty sure that the knife pricking him had broken the skin. He was more annoyed than scared, which he put down to a rush of adrenaline combined with an absence of working brain cells. "Okay, okay, don't give yourself an aneurysm. Did you bring a flashlight because I didn't get the chance?"

"Cheeky little bastard. Get moving." Fedora Man produced a flashlight and directed it at the walls as Landry walked back along the street searching for what he guessed should be a narrow alley. When he found it, he wasn't surprised that he and Gage had missed it. In the darkness it was all but invisible and, even with the flashlight, the shadows overlapped in a way that made it seem like the wall had no break. He found it by stumbling into the gap. Barely a shoulder-width wide, it was unlit. Landry ventured in a few paces, hesitant on the rough ground, until Fedora Man redirected the light at their feet. Landry discarded the scarf, which was hindering his progress by trailing on the floor. The path had to be two hundred yards long at least, skirting the building and the walled backyard of the pub. It ended in a steep flight of steps that disappeared toward the river. Landry could hear the gentle lapping of water below and there was a slight brackish scent in the air.

When he reached the base of the steps, pebbles shifted beneath his feet, becoming grittier closer to the water. A steep bank, dense with tangled vegetation backed the narrow strip of beach.

"It has to be under there somewhere," Landry said, more to himself than anything. He eyed the mass of foliage.

"So get looking."

Guessing that the tunnel wouldn't be close to where the path had been cut into the bank, Landry moved to the far end of the beach. Any further and he'd be in the water. Scrambling around with his hands in cuffs wasn't easy and the wavering, single beam of light guiding him didn't help much. The bank was thick with brambles, nettles and a dense tangle of shrubs, most of which seemed to have thorns as sharp as Fedora Man's knife.

"I don't suppose you brought a machete," Landry said. "Actually, strike that. I'd rather you didn't have one."

Below him on the beach, Fedora Man twirled his knife like a baton. In a moment of panic, Landry pictured him in a cheerleader's outfit, which made him snort with laughter.

"Get on with it!"

You get up here and try it! Landry carried on searching, cursing the vegetation. He was balancing on tiptoe, a bramble caught in his shirt, when he found a void behind a bush. "Point the light up here," he shouted. "I think I found something." The base of the tunnel was level with his eye line. He pushed some of the foliage aside as best he could and exposed an opening big enough for a man to crawl into, but not to stand.

"So you are good for something. Get in there."

The idea of crawling into the darkness wasn't enticing but it was preferable to being on the beach with a knife-wielding dude with anger issues. Landry lost some skin on his knees and elbows as he hauled himself up. Bits of stone around the lip of the tunnel crumbled away as he moved. Once he was in, Fedora Man tossed up the flashlight he'd been using.

The air hung heavy with the acrid scent of decay and damp. Water dripped incessantly from unseen crevices. Landry knelt in an inch of muck, cringing at the thought of what might be under his hands. *Gross. So gross.* The beam of light that the flashlight cut through the darkness illuminated brick walls covered in a sickly green patina. A wave of claustrophobia swept over him, and he had to take a few steadying breaths to stops himself from having a meltdown.

The tunnel stretched into the shadows, its curvature conspiring with the lack of light to conceal what lay beyond. He moved a few feet further and found rusted iron rungs ascending into a vertical shaft. Shadows danced on the walls, taking on sinister, malevolent shapes.

To Landry it seemed like the oppressive atmosphere thickened with every passing moment. "Are you going to tell me your secrets?" Landry whispered. "I think it's about time you gave them up, don't you?" He crawled further, gagging as he passed the well-rotted corpse of a rat. Every few inches he circled the tunnel with the torch, checking the bricks for any sign that something might be hidden. He wasn't sure how far he'd gone when he found it. Etched into a brick, just above his eye line, was the rough outline of three hens, drawn like crude stick figures. When he looked closely Landry could see that the mortar around the brick was of a different consistency to the rest of the tunnel. It had partly crumbled away and when he pulled at it there was movement.

He scraped around the edges of the brick with his fingers, not having anything else he could use, until finally he yanked it free. It came loose so suddenly that he toppled sideways, soaking one side of his body in viscous mud and green slime.

"There'd better be something in here," he grumbled. Where the brick had come loose there was a cavity in the wall of the tunnel. Landry had found something hidden behind a waterfall once. *This is way more disgusting. Plus, Gage was with me then. Now...I'm frightened.* He groped inside the hole, praying that it wasn't inhabited by hungry creepy-crawlies. He'd had to leave the flashlight on the ground and had to work by touch alone. His fingers came into contact with something soft, and he had to steel himself not to pull away.

Leather. It's a leather bag. Excited, despite his predicament, Landry pulled the bag free. He put it in his lap and struggled to unknot the drawstring around its neck. Once it was loose, he tipped the contents into his hands and grasped. The egg was stunning. It had been so well protected, it was clean and shiny. The jewels were brilliant, flashing in the torchlight. Landry found a little catch to open the egg and inside was a golden hen, and a tiny nest containing a brilliant blue jewel. "Wow."

"Get out here, right now!" Fedora Man was climbing into the tunnel.

Hurriedly Landry closed the egg and put it back in its bag before tucking it inside his waistband. He began to reverse crawl down the tunnel, which was too narrow for him to turn around fully. *He's going to stab me in the ass, I know he is.* Reversing felt vulnerable.

"I'm coming. Keep your hat on." When he reached the rusted rungs he'd spotted earlier, Landry made a split-second decision. He pulled himself upright and started to climb as fast as he could. He couldn't manage the flashlight and dropped it with a clatter. It went out, leaving him in pitch blackness, and he carried on climbing by touch.

"Get out here you little bastard! You're going to pay for making me come in here." The sounds of cursing and scrabbling were faint by the time they reached Landry's ears. He climbed faster then yelped as the top of his head connected with something solid. He'd reached the end of his escape route and, though he pushed upward, whatever was blocking the tunnel was immovable. He expected at any moment to feel a hand gripping his ankle, or the searing pain of a knife in his calf. Neither happened. Instead, an eerie silence, broken only by the drip of water, enveloped him. He took a few deep, shuddering breaths. The adrenaline that had kept him going so far was ebbing. Damp and cold were taking their toll and his hands cramped around the rungs.

"Landry? Landry, are you in here? It's Tad."

"Oh, thank fuck! I'm here." Landry clambered down the shaft slower than he'd gone up. The horizontal tunnel was now full of light, and Tad's head and shoulders were sticking through the entrance.

"Is it safe?" Landry asked.

"Would I be putting my head into this stinking hole if it wasn't?" Tad said. "Gage wanted to come get you, but his shoulders don't fit."

Landry giggled as he descended. He dropped to his knees then reverse crawled toward Tad.

"Keep coming, it's only a few more feet." Tad helped Landry until he could lie on his front with his legs dangling out of the hole then Tad moved out of the way, and Gage took over, pulling Landry into his arms. Landry clung to him like a limpet then burst into tears. "I was so scared!"

Gage carried him along to the steps then sat down with Landry on his lap. It was only then that Landry took a look around and realized that there were several people on the narrow strip of sand. Powerful torches lit the scene. Ellery was there, and Tad. Several uniformed policemen and a few men and women who he guessed were also cops but not in uniform also bustled around. Fedora Man now sported his own pair of handcuffs and was snarling in the grip of two extra-large cops.

"Can you get these off me?" Landry shook his wrists making the chain jangle.

One of the cops produced a key and, seconds later, Landry was rubbing his bruised skin. "Those are much more fun when they're fur-lined or padded."

The cop snorted with laughter and Gage groaned. "Really, you had to go there? I have to work with these people."

"Sorry? Hey, you're not going to punish me for this, are you? It wasn't my fault I got shoved in a car at knifepoint and brought down here."

"No, sweetheart, I should never have let you go find Winston on your own. He's mortified by the way that he got tricked into being distracted so easily. He said he was down the far end of the street and, even though he ran to help you, he wasn't fast enough."

"He shouldn't be upset. Scarface hat man over there told me that Winston has had him running all over London because of his false information. He might have nabbed me a lot sooner if it wasn't for Winston. We owe him a drink or three."

"We'll definitely sort that out. Now either you're inordinately pleased to see me, which I can understand, or there's something hard down the front of your pants."

Landry snickered. "I couldn't climb and carry it and it wouldn't fit in my pocket, so I had to shove it down my pants." He pushed a hand under his waistband then pulled out the leather pouch.

"I was about to tell you to keep it in your pants, Landry but I think I've changed my mind." Ellery had walked over to join them, Tad at his shoulder. "Is that what I think it is?"

Landry nodded. "Yeah, it is. You were right. It's real. The three hens showed the final hiding place, so Petey and the others get credit, too."

"You found it, it's yours."

"Don't be an idiot, Ellery. This was always your treasure hunt. We were just along for the ride, and I wouldn't dream of claiming it." He handed the pouch to Ellery.

Gently, Ellery emptied it into his hand. "You're a sweet boy and far too good to be my friend. I don't deserve you." He cradled the egg in his palm. "There was only ever a vague description of this. It's even more beautiful than I imagined. I've never seen so many rose-cut diamonds in one place. Why is it all muddy?"

"Uh, that would be my fault," Landry admitted. "Sorry?"

"You get a pass for the whole kidnapped at knifepoint thing."

"Thanks, I think."

Ellery fawned over the egg a bit more then opened it. "Would you look at that? That sapphire is stunning."

"What do you think it's worth?" Landry asked.

"Millions. It's priceless really, but collectors will fight over this."

"Shouldn't it be in a museum?"

"If they can pay for it." Ellery put the egg back in the leather bag. "We'll see."

"Won't the police want it?" Landry eyed the activity on the beach.

"When we realized you'd been taken, Gage called in his colleagues to track down a kidnapper. They don't know you found the egg and they don't need to."

Landry clambered off Gage's lap. "They don't? Gage, is that right?"

"They already know that this whole shit show is linked to a missing Russian treasure but they don't know you found it. They're more interested in bringing down Volkov for multiple murders and finding their leak. This is only the start of their investigation. I will have to tell them, though."

"But not today," Ellery said. "You need to take Landry back to the hotel and patch him up. Give him a bit of TLC. Tomorrow is soon enough to mention what he found."

Gage grunted. "Are you trying to make me your sidekick, because that's not gonna happen?"

"We make a great team," Ellery said.

"No."

Ellery gave him an enigmatic smile. Tad and Landry exchanged glances.

"I'm gonna talk to the Brits, see if it's okay to take you home, Lan," Gage said. Ellery went with him.

Landry sat on the steps again, his legs a bit shaky. Tad sat next to him and bumped knees.

"You were really brave. That tunnel was gross. And small!"

"I was more worried about what was going to happen if I came out," Landry said. "You guys got here right on time."

"Gage was about ready to tear down half of London. He kinda stole a car from outside the hotel."

"He what?"

"He yelled 'police!' and the driver let him take it, to be fair, but it was exciting. He drove, James rode shotgun and I was yelling directions from the back. He ground the gears a bit. Don't tell him I told you."

"He doesn't drive a stick that often."

"Is that a euphemism?" Tad asked, straight faced.

"Oh my God." Landry fell about laughing until his body reminded him of his various bruises and scrapes. "I need to spend about three hours soaking in a hot tub full of bubbles. They arrested fedora guy, I see."

"He was climbing into the tunnel after you. Gage dragged him out by his ankles then tossed him into a bramble bush. They got the two guys in the limo that brought you here, too. The police caught up with us outside Les Trois Poules and blocked the road."

"So you saw all the action while I got to crawl around in the muck."

"Pretty much."

"There was a dead rat in there, Tad."

"I wondered what that smell was. Didn't like to say anything."

"Oh God. You know, this really made me think about Frederick Ascott and the lengths he went to in hiding the egg. I wonder what was going through his head. Do you think someone was after him at the time?"

"It wouldn't surprise me. I don't know much about the history of that period but I guess a lot of stuff would have been taken by people escaping the new regime in Russia. He was grieving, too, so goodness knows what was going through his head. The clues he laid were detailed and clever. It was pure chance James came across that note. It could easily have been lost forever."

"James would have found the egg by himself eventually."

"I'm not so sure. He knew Volkov was on the egg's trail, too. If he hadn't had your help, and Gage's, and the crew back in Seattle when it comes to it, Volkov might have got there first. The egg would have disappeared out of the country and no doubt been sold for his benefit. The proceeds would have funded more of his criminal activities."

"This is going to make Ellery very rich, isn't it?" Landry said, "Do you think he'll retire?"

"He's already very rich, you've seen the apartment."

"True."

"Besides, can you picture James reclining on a chaise longue, with me on my knees feeding him grapes?"

Landry thought about it. "Actually, yes. You'd probably be naked..."

"With an enormous butt plug shoved up my ass." Tad chuckled. "Okay, bad example. But no, I can't imagine him stopping. He enjoys the danger, the adventure, the travel and the money. I don't know what he plans to do with the egg. He already has more than enough money."

"Diamond-encrusted chastity cage for you? Golden chains, the best silk blindfolds… No, I don't think that's his thing."

"Nor mine. They're coming back." Tad got up as Ellery and Gage arrived.

"We're good to go," Gage said. "They said you can give your statement in the morning. You can come into work with me."

"How are we getting back?" Landry asked.

"I already called a cab," Ellery said. "Gage is not allowed to hijack any more vehicles. I hope the hotel bar is still open."

"A bath and bed for you," Gage said to Landry.

"Sounds good, though I'm not sure I'll be able to sleep." Landry knew he'd be playing what happened over and over in his head.

"Don't worry, love, I'll make sure you're too exhausted to stay awake." Gage took Landry's hand and rubbed his thumb across Landry's palm.

Landry heaved himself upright. "That sounds perfect, Sir."

Epilogue

Ellery and Tad had disappeared from the hotel the day after the egg's discovery. A note shoved under the door of their room told Landry that the pair had returned to Ellery's Chelsea apartment and that they'd be in touch. Though a little upset at them leaving without saying goodbye, Landry could understand why they wanted to be alone together. He missed Tad's company while Gage was at work, but he'd enjoyed lounging in their room, reading, catching up with his friends in Seattle and sharing coffee and donuts with Winston.

A week later, Ellery had texted Gage to invite them for dinner at The Underground the next evening. All Landry's cuts and scrapes had healed, and he was more than ready for a night out. He'd treated himself to a shopping trip for a new outfit and was enjoying the hungry looks that Gage had been sending across the dinner table since they'd arrived.

"Those pants are obscene. I love them," Gage said. "I don't love that every guy in here had his eyes on your ass when you walked across the club."

Landry had found black pants in stretchy faux leather. They had a biker look with lots of stitched straps, rivets and rings. The zipper was silver and stood out rather than being concealed. It went from the waistband round to his ass, implying easy access. He'd paired them with a sleeveless black mesh shirt, the transparent material broken by matte black stripes so it wasn't too revealing for Gage. The high neck had a small stand-up collar and there was a full-length zipper down the front. Gage could have him naked in minutes if he wanted to.

"I don't think you've ever looked more fuckable."

Landry's face heated. "Aw, you're such an old romantic, Sir. You look hot, too." *Incendiary hot in all that leather.* "Just as many people were watching you." He'd had to give more than one wide-eyed sub a warning glance.

"They're late," Gage said. "I'm getting hungry."

Landry suspected he wasn't talking about the food. "Me, too." He blinked, keeping his expression innocent. "Starving. Here they are now."

Ellery pulled out a chair for Tad before taking a seat himself. "Sorry we're late, this one took an age to get dressed."

Landry was about to say something but thought better of it. Tad was only wearing a pair of skimpy leather shorts and chunky boots. He could have got dressed in about two minutes. He gave Gage a knowing glance. Gage shook his head. "Sure, Ellery, blame Tad. You're the one who needs all the work before he ventures out, not him."

Tad snorted with laughter. Ellery narrowed his eyes. "At least my razor was working, yours seems to have left two day's stubble. Besides, getting dressed wasn't what caused the delay."

"Yeah, we know all about those kinds of delays. You're here now. It's good to see you."

"And there's a line I never thought would come out of your mouth," Ellery said. "I knew I'd win you over eventually. I'm a very likable person."

"This surge of tolerance could disappear very easily," Gage said.

"Noted. I ordered iced water for all of us when we passed the bar. I wasn't sure what you two were planning for later, but Tad and I have a private room booked and you're very welcome to join us." Ellery grinned. "Gage, you okay? Only your face is going a bit purple." The server arrived with a large carafe of water and some glasses. Ellery poured a glass then handed it to Gage.

Landry was doing his best not to laugh. Tad was paying very careful attention to his napkin, but his shoulders were shaking.

"Keep it up, Landry. A bit of privacy to whip your behind might not be such a bad thing," Gage grumbled. "Stop encouraging him."

Landry's face heated. He wasn't averse to that idea at all.

"Tad, how about you give Gage and Landry their gifts," Ellery said. "I, we, wanted to give you both a souvenir of your trip, partly as a thank you and partly as an apology for dragging you into our little adventure."

"Little?" Landry mouthed at Gage.

"I want you to know that I appreciate your help. It was never my intention to put you in danger, but I was aware it was a possibility."

"*You* are a sneaky, manipulative pain in the rear," Gage said. "You're lucky everything turned out okay in the end because otherwise I would have to beat your ass for putting Landry in danger."

"Well, I'm not averse to the occasional spanking." Ellery held up his hands. "Joke!"

Tad held a wrapped box out to Landry. "Thanks for everything, Lan. This one's for you."

Landry cut his gaze to Gage who was scowling. *What can I do, it's a gift!* He tore the paper off the box then lifted the lid. Inside was a beautiful crystal lucky cat.

"For your collection. We wanted you to have something special to remember your trip."

"Gage?"

"It's lovely, Landry." Gage's expression softened.

"It is. It's absolutely beautiful." The problem? Landry was online a lot, looking at cats to add to his collection. Unless he missed his guess, this one was over five hundred dollars. There was no way he could accept it. He held the box back out to Tad.

"Thank you, but I couldn't possibly. It's too much."

"Oh, I'm sure Gage doesn't mind, do you, chum?" James asked, a bright smile on his face. "It's much less than you deserve, Landry."

"Go ahead and keep it, Lan. You've earned it." Gage gave him a reassuring smile.

"I love it!" Landry stroked the crystal, admiring the delicate feline features etched on the glass. He looked at the base and revised his estimate of the cat's value. "But, this is Lalique!"

"Only the best for you," Ellery said.

Tad handed another package to Gage. "And this is for you."

Gage unwrapped his box. He lifted out a solid blue glass butt plug with a bulbous, spherical tip, a slim neck and wide, anchor-shaped base. "This has Lalique on the bottom, too. How the hell did you manage that?"

Ellery grinned. "Connections. You can be assured that there's no other like it."

"I don't know what to say."

"Me either," Landry added, eyeing the sizable plug.

"It's not one for beginners," Ellery said. "Of course, you might want to use it on yourself, Gage. Landry looks a little apprehensive."

Landry fell about laughing. "Oh, Ellery, you really like to skate on the edge of survival, don't you?"

"Fuck you, Ellery, but thanks." Gage raised his water glass in a toast. "Here's to none of us getting dead. Even Ellery."

The toast was followed by ordering food and then much laughter while they ate. Landry was excited to be back at The Underground and felt much more able to fully enjoy the atmosphere now that Ellery was safely back where he belonged.

"I love this place. Everyone is so welcoming."

Tad smirked. "You bet they are when you come in dressed like that."

"You can talk! You're barely dressed at all," Landry retorted.

"I know, hot, isn't it?"

"Are you talking about you or the temperature?"

Tad pressed his chilled water glass against his cheek in response.

"Scorch is good too," Gage said, defending the BDSM club he and Landry went to in Seattle. "Just a bit less refined."

"I don't need refined," Landry said, "I just need people around me I love."

"Well you have that, sweetheart." Gage patted Landry's knee beneath the table.

"What are you guys going to do with the rest of your stay in England?" Tad asked.

"Once his stint in London is up, Gage has international conference thingies in Manchester and York," Landry said. "We want to visit Canal Street in Manchester and hopefully fit in a night at Collars and Cuffs while we're there. Then in York, I want to do a ghost walk and see the Minster and explore all the quaint old alleyways and…"

"It sounds like you're going to be busy," Ellery said. "I can make some calls and get you a guest pass to Collars and Cuffs. How about when all the work commitments are over?"

"We'll only have a few days before we fly back to Seattle from London, so we thought we'd meander south from York, find some cute B&Bs and explore a few places along the way. Landry has a thing for castles."

"England is bristling with those," Tad said. "I can recommend Richmond Castle and I like Baddesley Clinton, which is a bit smaller, if you can get there."

"Ooh, I read about that one," Landry said. "There are priest holes there."

Gage groaned. "I'd really appreciate a quiet life for a while, Lan. No more mysteries or adventures, okay? I'd have thought you'd had enough of dark holes in the ground for now."

"Anyone would think I invited trouble," Landry muttered, "and I so don't."

"The only way to keep you *out* of trouble is to chain you to the bed," Gage said, eliciting a broad grin from Ellery. "Say nothing if you know what's good for you, Ellery."

"What's next for you, Ellery?" Landry thought it might be wise to change the subject. "Happy retirement on some Caribbean island?"

"Much as I enjoy seeing Tad in very little, I have an aversion to sand," Ellery said with a grimace. "That stuff reaches parts of the body it has no business getting to."

"Something we actually agree on," Gage said.

"But sandcastles are fun! And rock pools and beach games and picnics…" Landry had to defend the beach. "So what then?"

"I already have my next job lined up as it happens. A rather nice Monet has gone walkabout from a Parisian gallery, so Tad and I will be taking a romantic break in the city of love. Do you fancy extending your trip to take in our European neighbors by any chance?"

"No!" Gage snapped. "We would not."

"I'd love to see Paris," Landry said, "but I miss home. I want to get back to Treasure Trove. Petey and Sorrel need me."

Ellery smiled. "I can understand that. You have a great life over there."

"What about the egg, what's happening with that?" Landry leaned forward, keen to hear about the treasure.

"In this country, if you find property that was lost or abandoned, the person who found it gets to keep it unless the original owner claims it. Basically, it's finders keepers. In this case the owner would have been Frederick Ascott and his heirs may have had a claim but as they are all dead that doesn't apply. There would have been a strong case for abandonment anyway."

"So the egg belongs to Landry," Gage said, his eyes glinting. "He found it."

"Gage, don't be naughty! I only found it because I got myself kidnapped. Again." Landry tilted his head to one side like a puppy. "Ellery did all the hard work and nearly got killed for his trouble."

"Thank you, Landry, that's kind. I'll be putting the egg up for sale and believe it or not, donating a good portion of the proceeds to charity, which is entirely due to your influence, after a generous cut for me. The price will be within reach of museum fundraisers because I'd rather it got to see the light of day rather than being hidden away again. I'd like you to suggest a suitable charity, if you have one you're fond of."

"You're getting soft in your old age. It suits you." Gage shook his head. "You'll be able to add some nice new toys to that playroom of yours."

"Less of the old, and I do have expenses and standards to maintain. I'll also be able to book some first-class flights to Seattle every now and again. If your government sees fit to let me back into the country, that is."

Gage groaned. "Fuck. I wonder if I can find any contacts in immigration…"

"Be nice, Sir!" Landry scolded. "We all know you like Ellery really."

"Do not."

"Do so!"

Gage was the first to look away, which made Landry smile inside. "I really wanna dance, Sir, can I?" Landry gazed at the packed dance floor and its crowd of undulating bodies.

"Me too!" Tad said.

"It might do them good to work off a bit of excess energy," Ellery observed. "Makes for a more pliable sub later."

Gage didn't seem convinced but relented after an extra dose of puppy eyes. "Okay but stay where we can see you."

"Yay!" Landry grabbed Tad's hand and the two of them headed right for the mob of happy dancers.

"We are two very lucky men," Ellery said, sipping his drink. "Landry is a delight.

"And Tad is exactly the challenge you need." Gage shifted his chair so he could maintain a better view of Landry.

"Tad won't let him get into any trouble. You don't need to worry."

"I always worry, that's part of being a Dom, isn't it?"

"I guess so."

"And on that note, there's something you've been holding back, isn't there? I can tell." Gage gave Ellery a hard stare. "I'd guess it has something to do with Anatoly Volkov."

"Hmm, you're more perceptive than you look. No offense."

"There's the potential for offense every time you open your mouth, Ellery, I'm used to it."

Ellery grinned. "Like I said, we make a great team." He looked thoughtful, as if debating something in his head. "I considered keeping this to myself but there's a small chance that it could rebound on you and Landry so..."

"Spill it, Ellery."

Ellery handed over a folded piece of paper he'd extracted from a pocket. "This was in the mailbox at my flat."

Gage read the message, which was handwritten in block capitals. The indentations on the paper were deep, as if the writer had been angry when writing and had exerted some force. He read aloud. "You win this time. My consolation is that you have a memento of our jousting. I look forward to our next meeting with anticipation. V." Gage handed the note back to Ellery. "He really doesn't like you, does he?"

"Apparently not."

"The Met confirmed he left the country. The flight plan filed was for Belarus, but he could have hopped several countries since then. He could be anywhere."

"He could, and that includes the States. We both need to be vigilant, though to be fair I don't think Volkov is the type for petty revenge. He'll wait until I'm on the hunt for something else he wants."

"Which means you won't be involving us. I mean it, Ellery. Keep Landry out of your scheming in future, or Volkov will be the least of your worries."

"Love it when you get all protective." Ellery smirked.

"How *is* your back? Will you have scars?"

"Nothing major, just lines when it's completely healed. It's no big deal. So you know, I'll be sending Landry a cut of the profits on the egg." He held up a hand to stop Gage speaking. "I'm telling you because I know he'd refuse, but he earned the money. What he does with it is up to him. A nest egg, donate to more charities, buy you a sense of humor... I'll mail the check to you when the time comes."

"You live to cause me grief, don't you?"

"You're fun to rile. I think it's time I treated Tad to a little special attention. The invitation to join us was genuine."

Gage shook his head. "Tempting, but I don't think so."

Ellery shrugged. "Worth a try. One day, I'll catch you at a weak moment."

"Fuck's sake. Dance floor, now. Before I choose violence."

There were a lot of tearful hugs as Landry said his goodbyes on the edge of the dance floor. Ellery even hugged Gage and Landry caught him hugging Ellery back. But eventually, Ellery towed Tad toward the private rooms, leaving them alone.

"I'm gonna miss them," Landry sniffled.

"Pretty sure it won't be the last we see of them, love. Not sure how I feel about that. How's about a bit of dance floor smooching with your Dom?"

"Ooh, yes please!"

Gage put his arms around Landry, holding him tight. They swayed together, not really dancing but keeping time with the music. Around them, the other dancers gave them a bit of space, as if sensing their need for their own little bubble.

"Nice and close, where I know you're safe," Gage murmured in Landry's ear.

"I'm always safe with you but wouldn't life be boring without a bit of excitement?"

"I could do without the kind of excitement Ellery brings to the party." Gage slipped a hand down the back of Landry's pants.

"I know you like him, even though you think you shouldn't. Oh!" Landry finished his sentence with a happy squeak.

"Not admitting to anything. No more talk of Ellery or jeweled eggs because there are wicked things I want to do to your ass." Gage pushed his finger into Landry's crack. "These pants are too tight."

"Maybe you should unzip them then." Landry pressed his body against Gage's, letting him know that his cock was hard and eager.

"This place turns you into a wanton little slut, doesn't it?"

"There's something in the air. I really want to sit on your cock, Sir."

Fuck, the things he does to me without even knowing. Gage pulled his hand out of Landry's pants so he could lift him up. Landry held on tight, and Gage carried him to a vacant booth in a dark corner. He nudged the table to one side to give them space. Landry knelt on the seat so that Gage could lower his zipper.

"There's a bowl of lube packets on the table, Lan, can you reach?" With a few contortions, Landry snagged a sachet. Before he handed it over, Gage tackled Landry's pants, unzipping them from ass to crotch. Landry held his butt above Gage's erection.

"Need you so bad!"

Gage didn't care that he got lube everywhere providing enough of it landed on his dick. "Ready?" He gripped Landry's waist, intending to lower him in gentle increments but Landry was having none of it. He slammed down with a happy cry then proceeded to bounce with enthusiastic abandon.

"Fuck, Landry, you're going to kill me." Gage had to brace himself with one arm on his seat. *But what a way to go.* Landry's cries were attracting attention. "Your ass is on view, love."

"Don't care!" Landry was panting, his eyes wide and lips parted. He made a grab for his bobbing cock, missed, cursed then tried again. "Eureka!" The sight of

Landry coming meant Gage had no hope of holding off. Landry kept moving while Gage came but finally drew to a shuddering stop. He sank onto Gage's lap, still impaled even as Gage softened inside him, and rested his forehead on Gage's shoulder. There was a smattering of applause as their audience realized the show was over. Gage placed his hands over Landry's exposed backside, making Landry giggle.

"It's a bit late for that, isn't it?"

"They've had all the free entertainment they're going to get from us tonight. Do up that zipper." Landry lifted himself from Gage's cock then zipped up. "Should have brought a plug. Gonna want in there again later."

"Oh, you will, huh?" Landry sat sideways on Gage's lap, arms around his neck.

"Yeah. Several times."

"Ambitious!"

Gage kissed him. "This trip has been quite a ride, hasn't it?"

"Well *that* just was, but yeah, not what I was expecting from my first visit to England, that's for sure."

"It'll be good to have some time for us. I meant what I said about the collar the last time we were here. I want us to choose something together when we get home."

Landry wiggled. "That would make me so happy."

"I want us to choose something else as well." Gage twisted a lock of Landry's hair around his finger, his mouth suddenly dry.

"Okay, whatever you want." Landry kissed his neck.

"How do you feel about rings?"

Landry almost fell off Gage's lap. "Are you, is that, did you just…?"

"Marry me, Landry Carran? Wear my collar *and* my ring. I want you to be mine always."

"Oh my God, yes!" Landry burst into tears, buried his face against Gage's shirt and soaked it through.

"Those are happy tears, right?"

"Yes, yes, yes, yes, yes!" Landry peppered Gage's face with kisses. A server appeared with a bottle of champagne in an ice bucket.

"With the compliments of Mr. James Ellery, sirs." He left it on the table along with two champagne flutes.

"How did he know?" Landry glanced around.

"The walls have ears in here. You want to toast our future, even though the bubbles tickle your nose?" Gage asked as he popped the cork. He shifted Landry onto the seat next to him before pouring two glasses. Landry immediately stuck his nose into the top of his and got a fit of the giggles. "Yes!"

Gage raised his glass. "To us. To a future together with no more life-risking escapades."

"To being yours and to love."

Lead crystal chimed as they clinked their glasses together. Landry sighed. "This night couldn't have been more perfect."

Gage took in the site of Landry's blissed-out expression. "No, no it couldn't, love."

Want to see more from this author?
Here's a taster for you to enjoy!

Family Business:
Thunderclouds and Sunshine
L.M. Somerton

Excerpt

Up to his elbows in soap suds, Alfie eyed the pile of dirty pans stacked on the work surface next to him. "At least I won't be out of a job anytime soon." He bopped around as much as his workstation would allow, humming along to the country tunes on the radio. His corner of the restaurant's basement kitchen was away from the food prep areas but there was a rhythm to the place. The chef yelling, serving staff complaining and the constant percussion of metal utensils banging against pots and pans. The heat was intense, and Alfie had learned on his first day not to wear too much. He had on a thin T-shirt, shorts and runners. All soaked with dirty pan water.

"How are you always so cheerful, Alfie?" Brent, the restaurant manager, stopped by on his regular route checking on all the staff. Alfie liked him because he genuinely cared about everybody.

"It's a good day! I have a job, a place to sleep and Chef saves me leftovers. Even the dish soap bubbles have little rainbows in them, look!" Alfie scooped some foam onto his finger. The bubbles were mesmerizing.

"Yeah, that's…great, I guess. What time are you on 'til tonight?"

"Midnight. Chloe called in sick."

"That's a long shift. Make sure to take a break."

"I will. I can use the extra money."

"That never changes. I'll catch you later." Brent headed for the freight elevator and Alfie went back to his pans.

By midnight, the racket had quieted and most of the staff had left for the night. Alfie cleaned up his station, grabbed the brown bag of goodies Chef Paolo had left him, then made his way to the back stairs. He was grateful that he only had to get to the attic to get home. His bedsit was tiny, but he'd made it as cozy as he could with thrift store finds and donations from kind coworkers. He had his own shower which, though cranky, produced plentiful hot water, and a kitchen cubby big enough to house a fridge, sink and microwave. His bed even had a new mattress, a soft comforter and lots of squishy pillows. It was enough for him and a huge bonus for central New York.

On the ground level, Alfie paused to look through the door into the restaurant. The window was round like a porthole and Alfie liked to think of the whole business as a ship, with the staff as crew and him as the cabin boy. There were lights on in part of the room and Alfie could see a group of men sitting around a table. They seemed relaxed, with drinks in hand. Alfie spotted Mr. Borroni, the restaurant's owner, deep in conversation. The enigmatic Italian had given Alfie a chance when he most needed it and Alfie would be forever grateful to him for that. At his shoulder, in the shadows, stood Mr. Borroni's assistant, Luca. Luca was the most handsome man Alfie had ever laid eyes on. Luca made Alfie's mouth go dry and induced tingling sensations in his groin. He had black hair, short but with a slight curl at the ends. His eyes were storm gray when they weren't hidden behind dark glasses. Alfie had never seen him smile.

What I'd let that man do to me. Alfie drifted into his most regular daydream. *Anything he wanted, as many times as he wanted. He could hold me down, I wouldn't be able to escape, then he could...* "Oh!" The swing door banged open and he narrowly avoided falling on his ass as he took a few rapid steps back.

"I thought I saw you out here, Alfie." All six feet four gorgeous inches of Luca Talete loomed over Alfie.

"Hey, Luca, I wasn't spying, honest. I saw the light and took a peek."

"It's late. You should be tucked up in bed by now."

Yes, please! With you. Naked. "I worked an extra shift."

Luca didn't seem pleased. "Are they working you too hard down there? I can have a word with Brent." He managed to sound threatening without effort.

"Oh no. Brent is always checking on me. It's just that Chloe called in sick and they couldn't get anyone else at such short notice and I didn't mind because washing pots is all part of a brilliant service."

"You've been listening to Mr. Borroni's motivational staff talks, haven't you?"

"Uh-huh." Alfie nodded. "He's right. Everyone plays their part, even me."

"Yours is an important part," Luca said. "You must be tired, but we're out of ice. Would you mind running down to the freezer for some more? I'd go myself, but I can't leave Mr. Borroni."

"Of course I can!" Alfie bounced, happy to be able to help Luca with something. "I'll be right back." He left his bag on the stairs then skipped down to the kitchen.

He filled a bucket with ice from the huge bin in one of the walk-in freezers, then carted it back up the stairs. He hovered at the door but no one came, so he plucked up his courage and took the ice into the restaurant. He was very aware of his state of dress and horrified when Mr. Borroni noticed him.

"Gentlemen, I'd like you to meet Alfie. He works in my kitchen here and does an excellent job."

Alfie stared at the carpet and the toes of his scuffed runners with one loose lace. "Hello," he managed to whisper.

"You're all intimidating the boy," Mr. Borroni scolded. "Thank you for the ice, Alfie."

There was a chorus of thank-yous and Alfie dared to peek from beneath his lashes. Everyone was smiling. No one seemed angry with him. He breathed a little easier and put the ice bucket on the table. "My pleasure," he murmured. Luca caught his eye and gave him the nod to leave.

Happy to be heading for his bed at last, Alfie skipped toward the door, forgetting that he needed to retie his lace. He tripped but managed to avoid falling headlong, instead dropping to his knees. He grappled with the lace but a flashing red light caught his eye. *What's that?* Ducking lower, he peered beneath the table he'd knelt next to. There was a small black box attached to its underside. It had a couple of switches and one ominous light, blinking steadily.

"Luca! There's a bomb!" Alfie yelled, launching himself back in the direction of Mr. Borroni and his guests.

Luca didn't hesitate. He bundled Mr. Borroni to the nearest exit and burst out onto the street. His guests followed, drinks abandoned and chairs toppled.

Alfie didn't know how long he had, only that he had to get out. To follow Luca. His limbs wouldn't cooperate. *I have to be wrong. I wouldn't know a bomb from a lump of cheese, except cheese doesn't have wires and red flashing lights. Why would anyone want to blow up an Italian restaurant? The food's so good at Borroni's!* He slipped, falling to one knee, but that allowed him to push off and gain some momentum like a sprinter from his blocks. Alfie threw himself toward the doors. He was pushing through them when the detonation happened. There was a moment's silence then a deafening roar. He was tossed through the air like a rag doll, heat searing his bare legs and arms.

Each heartbeat took an eternity as the ground rushed to meet him. He hit asphalt with a bone-jarring impact. His vision darkened for a second or two but he wasn't granted the mercy of unconsciousness. He lay where he'd landed, nostrils filled with the acrid stench of burning debris. The distant wail of sirens competed with the crackle of fire. Sharp snaps and pops punctured the air, accompanied by the hiss of evaporating moisture and the snapping of timbers.

A small explosion made Alfie's heart leap. *Gas canister in the kitchen.* His eyes were stinging and watering from the smoke. Beneath his hands, sharp splinters jabbed at his skin. He dragged himself to his knees, peering through the smoke, the scene now illuminated by flashing lights from approaching emergency vehicles. There were figures moving in his direction but to one side a man stood watching. Not helping, just observing with clinical detachment. He caught Alfie's eye, scowled, then melted away into the darkness.

Alfie coughed and once he started, he couldn't stop. He needed to get to cleaner air but couldn't summon the will to move.

"Alfie, how badly are you hurt? Can I pick you up?"

Luca. "I...don't know. My ears... I don't think anything's too bad." Alfie blinked in an attempt to clear his watering eyes. Luca's face was smoke blackened, and blood ran from a small cut that dissected his eyebrow. He looked grim. Alfie shifted and pain shot through his wrist. "Oh! My wrist... I think it might be broken."

Luca scooped him off the ground with no apparent effort, taking care not to jostle his arm. "You saved a lot of lives tonight, Alfie. Everyone in that restaurant owes their continued existence to you."

"I just yelled. Why would anyone want to blow up Borroni's, Luca? I don't understand."

"Not something for you to worry about. Let's get you fixed up." Luca carried Alfie through a sea of debris, chunks of brick and shards of glittering glass. An ambulance had pulled up a short distance away, with more approaching. Bystanders were helping where they could.

"Are other people hurt?" Alfie asked. "Is Mr. Borroni okay?"

"He's absolutely fine. A couple of the others have minor cuts. You were last out and closest to the blast."

"It was loud, and hot. Then I was on the floor."

"Your limbs are all still attached. That's good. Did you hit your head?"

"I don't think so. It's going to be tough to wash pots with one arm, though." The realization of what had happened started to sink in. "But I guess I don't have a job now, or a home!" For the first time, tears welled. "Everything I owned was in that building." Alfie craned his neck to look back at the restaurant. The building was fully alight, firefighters directing jets of water at the roof. It appeared to be a lost cause.

"Don't look."

"What am I gonna do?" Alfie wailed, tears rolling down his cheeks.

"You're going to let the guys here look you over and not worry about anything else for now." Luca deposited Alfie in the back of an ambulance. "Fix him up." The 'or else' was implied.

Alfie submitted to the ministrations of two eager paramedics who did a thorough job of checking him over before declaring that he needed to go to the hospital.

"Should we tell your friend?" one of them asked. "Only he seemed…protective."

"I guess." Alfie didn't want to bother Luca, but he wanted someone to know where he was. The only reason he didn't panic about hospital bills was because his ears were still ringing and he was in enough pain to be distracted. One of the ambulance crew got him settled and strapped to a gurney while the other went to update Luca.

A few minutes later, the rig pulled away and Alfie let his eyes drift shut. He'd had a long day, a traumatic night and now, in the early hours, all he wanted to do was sleep. Of course, the paramedic riding in back with him wouldn't let him.

The rest of the night passed in a blur of examinations and treatment. Alfie had first degree burns on the backs of his arms and legs, multiple small cuts, and a hairline fracture to his left wrist. The nurses and doctors were kind, but Alfie didn't want to be admitted.

"Do I need to sign anything?" he asked. "I have to go." He sat on the edge of the bed in the ER in the remains of his tattered clothes.

"I'd prefer to admit you for twenty-four hours at least," the doctor said.

Luca pushed through the curtain. "You're in no condition to go anywhere, Alfie. You need to be observed, so do as the doctor tells you."

Alfie gulped, his throat still raw. "But, I…"

"Your bills are covered. Do as you're told." Luca pinned him with a gaze that dared him to disobey.

"I… Okay, but how?"

"You're Mr. Borroni's employee. He cares about you. He insisted that you get everything you need. Once you're discharged, you'll be staying at his estate in North Salem until we work out a plan for your future." Luca glared. "Any objections?"

"No, Luca," Alfie replied meekly. He didn't really understand what was going on or why Mr. Borroni would be so generous. *I'll find a way to pay him back but I really need to sleep first.*

Alfie wasn't considered well enough to walk anywhere. A porter by the name of Jimmy wheeled him all the way to a private room on the top floor of the hospital. The room had its own bathroom and, despite his fatigue, Alfie was desperate for a shower. He reeked of smoke and his skin was coated in grime and blood, apart from in the patches that had been cleaned up for treatment. The doctor had decided not to put his wrist in plaster but it was still heavily strapped. Jimmy helped him off the trolley.

"Is it okay if I take a shower?" Alfie asked.

"I'll have to fetch a nurse. They'll want you to cover up your wrist. I'm not an expert but I know that much. Gimme five." He turned to Luca. "Are you staying, sir? Someone needs to be here to watch him if he's not horizontal."

Luca gave a curt nod. "Not going anywhere."

"I really need to use the bathroom, Luca. I can manage."

"Leave the door open. You feel dizzy or faint, you yell. I don't want you falling on your ass."

"You must have more important things to do than stay here with me," Alfie said as he made his way carefully to the toilet.

"Nope."

That's all I'm gonna get? Alfie did his business and by the time he was decent, the porter had returned with a nurse.

"This is Marsha," Jimmy said. "She's the best nurse in the hospital and she's gonna take care of you real good. You get better now, ya hear."

Jimmy left and Alfie offered Marsha a tentative smile. She beamed right back.

"Well look at the state of you, honey. I think we should get you cleaned up and then you can rest."

"Oh, yes please. I'm so stinky."

"Well, I didn't like to say." Marsha let out a belly laugh that made Alfie smile. "Now I have kids and grandkids and there ain't much I haven't seen, but if you prefer, your friend can help you undress and watch you in the shower while I wait out here. I have a plastic wrap for that arm. Your other dressings will be fine and then I can reapply burn cream before you go to sleep."

Alfie was so desperate to get clean, he was past caring who he had to get naked in front of, but Luca stepped forward. "You can leave him with me. He'll be safe."

Marsha looked Luca up and down, completely unintimidated. He apparently passed muster because she nodded. "Yes, I think he will. I'll get you some scissors to cut his clothes off and a garbage bag to put them in. Sorry, Alfie, but they're beyond redemption."

Marsha produced the necessary equipment. She wrapped Alfie's arm. "There's a fold-down seat in the shower. Use it."

"Yes, ma'am." Marsha was almost as fearsome as Luca.

"Good answer. I'll give you ten minutes then I'll be back to get you safely into bed." She gave Luca a thoughtful glance. "I'll bring a pillow and some blankets for you. The chair reclines a bit. It's not comfortable, but it won't kill you."

Luca is going to stay the night? Not that there's much of the night left.

"Bathroom, Alfie," Luca ordered.

Alfie gulped, his pain-muddled brain registering that he now had to get naked in front of his crush. *With any luck I'll faint in there and not know anything about it.*

About the Author

LM lives in a small village in the English countryside, surrounded by rolling hills, cows and sheep. She started writing to fill time between jobs and is now firmly and unashamedly addicted.

She loves the English weather, especially the rain, and adores a thunderstorm. She loves good food, warm company and a crackling fire. She's fascinated by the psychology of relationships, especially between men, and her stories contain some subtle leanings towards BDSM.

LM is a past winner of the National Leather Association – International's Pauline Reage Award for best novel and John Preston award for short fiction. She has twice won the Golden Flogger Award for best BDSM novel in the LGBT category. She has received multiple Honorable Mentions in the Rainbow Awards and won the Action and Adventure category of Divine Magazine's Book Awards.

LM loves to hear from readers. You can find her contact information, website details and author profile page at https://www.firstforromance.com/

Sign up for our newsletter and find out about all our romance book releases, eBook sales and promotions, sneak peeks and FREE romance books!

www.ingramcontent.com/pod-product-compliance
Lightning Source LLC
Chambersburg PA
CBHW020826260626
47169CB00003B/855